A PUBLISHER'S NOTE

To my dearest readers:

Triple Crown Publications provides you with the best reads in hip-hop fiction. Each novel is hand-selected in its purest form with you, the reader, in mind. *Let That Be the Reason*, an insta-classic, pioneered the hip-hop genre. Always innovative, you can count on Triple Crown's growth: manuscript notes — published books — audio — film.

Triple Crown has also gone international, with novels distributed around the globe. In Tokyo, the books have been translated into Japanese. Triple Crown's revolutionary brand has garnered attention from prominent news media, with features in ABC News, *The New York Times*, *Newsweek*, MTV, *Publisher's Weekly*, *The Boston Globe*, *Vibe*, *Essence*, *Entrepreneur magazine*, *Inc magazine*, *Black Enterprise magazine*, *The Washington Post*, *Millionaire Blueprints magazine* and *Writer's Digest*, just to name a few. I recently earned Ball State University's Ascent Award for Entrepreneurial Business Excellence and was named by Book Magazine as one of publishing's 50 most influential women. Those prestigious honors have taken me from street corner to boardroom accreditation.

Undisputedly, Triple Crown is the leader of the urban fiction renaissance, boasting more than one million sizzling books sold and counting...

Without you, our readers, there is no us,

Vickie Stringer
Publisher

The Pink Palace II
MONEY, POWER, & SEX

BY

MARLON MCCAULSKY

Compilation and Introduction copyright © 2010 by
Triple Crown Publications
PO Box 247378
Columbus, Ohio 43224
www.TripleCrownPublications.com

Library of Congress Control Number: 2010928988
ISBN 13: 978-0-9825888-3-3

Author: Marlon McCaulsky
Graphics Design: Valerie Thompson, Leap Graphics
Photography: Treagen Kier
Editor-in-Chief: Vickie Stringer

First Trade Paperback Edition Printing 2010

10 9 8 7 6 5 4 3 2 1

Printed in the United States of America

Dedicated to

Haiti, be strong. Jamaica, one love.

Prologue

Back again for the first time

Atlanta, GA
NICOLE "NIKKI" BELL

It had been three years since I had been back at The
Pink Palace. It felt like a lifetime ago. I'm a different
person now than I was back then. Back then you couldn't
tell me nothing. I was hustling these tricks, shaking my
ass and selling my body to the man with the most cash.
I was doing anything and everything for the dollar. God,
I was so stupid.

It wasn't until I got caught up in my own hustle, got
my ass kicked by a nigga who didn't give a shit about
me and almost died as a result of my stupid state of
mind did I realize how foolish I was being and changed

my life. So you ask why am I back here? Because less than a month ago my whole world was ripped apart and now I gotta do what I gotta do in order to protect the man I love.

After I quit stripping three years ago I started to live my life with the man I loved with all my heart, Andre Wade. Dre had quit the game too and started his own business in midtown called A-Town Grillz. Most importantly, we had a baby boy named Tyler. He changed everything for us. I became a mother and Dre was going to be the father to Tyler that he never had. We were starting to live our lives together and bought a house in the Stone Ridge subdivision in College Park. We decided to take our time and plan the wedding that I never thought I would have.

My cousin Janelle, whom I loved dearly, was going to be my maid of honor. She was going to be mine, like I had been her maid of honor when she got married to Jayson. I was so proud of her. Janelle had always been the strongest of us. I never told her this but she always inspired me to do better. I wondered what she would think if she saw me here now? But at any rate, life was going perfect, or that's what I thought, until Dre started to receive mysterious phone calls. He always seemed to be upset after he got off the phone so I finally decided to ask him about it.

"Dre, baby ... what's going on?"

He smiled, "It's nothing baby."

"It didn't sound like nothing. Who's been calling you?"

"Nobody important. Just some niggas I used to run with back in the day," Dre coolly replied, as he picked Tyler up off the couch where he fell asleep.

"What do they want?"

"Like I said, nothing important," Dre told me again as he took Tyler to his room and laid him down in his crib. "The only thing I'm looking forward to is getting your pretty behind down to Miami this weekend."

Whatever it was, Dre didn't want to talk about it and I didn't want to push and start a fight right before we went on a mini vacation to South Beach. Besides, if Dre didn't want to talk about something he wasn't gonna talk about it.

"Okay, well remember Penny said she'd watch Tyler for us. I don't know how she's gonna deal with Tyler and her bad ass little Tarius. But she said it's no problem," I told him.

"Good, our flight leaves at 12:30 tomorrow so we'll drop him off at nine." Dre saw a concerned expression on my face. "Nikki, you don't got anything to worry about okay."

"Okay baby but you know you can tell me anything … I love you."

"I know Nikki and I love you too." He kissed my lips.

I know Dre hadn't gone back to hustling but he still knew people in the game. He's even told me that the money we make from A-Town Grillz was more than enough and he didn't need to hustle anymore. Between selling custom grills and jewelry, CD's and a small fashion boutique I run, we were able to buy our house in College Park.

In my heart I knew there was something else going on that Dre wasn't telling me. I decide not to press the issue and just concentrate on enjoying myself in Miami with my man. We packed our suitcases that night and the next day we headed over to Penny's house in Morrow. She still stayed in the same house Janelle and I used to stay in with her. Penny quit dancing at The Pink Palace a year ago and I hired her at our store.

After we dropped Tyler off, we drove to Hartsfield-Jackson Atlanta International Airport and we were off to Miami. After I had Tyler, Dre made it a point for us to take mini vacations together so we wouldn't get caught up in just living life but also enjoyed it. We had the money so why not?

We got to Miami two hours later. Dre rented us a 2011 Lexus Coupe and we drove down Ocean Drive to The Regent Hotel. Once we got settled, I enjoyed the beautiful view of the beach from the balcony of our lavish suite. Dre was doing it big for me and that's why I loved him so much.

"This is what I needed," I told him as I stood and stared out at the blue water. Dre walked up behind me and put his arms around my waist.

"And you're all I need right here." His big hands began rubbing my breasts.

I leaned my head back and kissed him. "You're all I ever needed baby."

"You wanna go down there?" Dre asked, nodding toward the beach.

"Yeah, I want to show you my new bikini."

"I can't wait to see you in it," Dre replied eagerly. He went back inside and changed into a pair of black shorts and flip-flops then went down to the lobby to wait for me. I changed into my exclusive, blue, Mychael Knight two-piece bikini. I was still shocked at how well my body got back into shape after I had Tyler. It was like I never had a baby. In fact my breasts went up a couple of sizes after I had him and it helped me fill out my bikini top to a tee. After I got dressed, I took the elevator down to the lobby and when the door opened I stepped off and Dre's eyes lit up.

"Sweet Jesus! Nikki you look ... wow," Dre droned.

"Just the reaction I was hoping for."

"Girl, I'm scared to take you out there."

"No need to be. I'm all yours."

We headed out to the beach, and just like Dre feared, all eyes were on me. Guys watched me walk on the powdery sand and my bikini showed all my sexy curves from my incredible eye popping cleavage, long brown legs to my round ass that bounced to its own beat. I wasn't the only one getting stared at though. Women were ogling Dre like the beefcake he was. His sexy muscular chest and six-pack were hard enough to lick whipped cream off of. But I had to admit the women on South Beach were gorgeous.

I even caught Dre sneaking a peek at a couple of Jamaican chicks. I couldn't even get mad at him cause they were stunning. It was a good thing we didn't live here or I'd have to fight a chick everyday!

Later that night Dre took me to a nightclub called Club B.E.D. If a man couldn't get a woman in bed there then he should just stop trying all together. The atmosphere in the club was young and sexy and I was the sexiest woman in the spot. I wore a sexy red spaghetti strapped dress, matching Prada shoes and my MAC makeup was flawless. Dre was pimped out in black Avirex Jeans and an all over silver Avirex logo printed polo. He was laced with his long platinum chain, iced out Rolex and his Atlanta fitted on his head.

Dre ordered us some Patron. The club was filled with ballers making it rain on pretty women and hustlers flossin' their ice. The DJ dropped Usher's "Love In This Club" and that's what it looked like everybody was doing on the dance floor as the women grinded on the men. I had no choice but to put it on Dre in my own special way. The club had plush, soft beds, and I made Dre lay back as I straddled and rode him like a jockey. I grinded my hips back and forth in a sexy saunter giving him a preview of what he was going to get later tonight.

"Oh shit, Nikki," Dre exclaimed as I felt his dick become rock hard underneath me. "You gonna make me tear your ass up right here in this club!"

"Well, we are on a bed ... and it wouldn't be the first time we've made love in a club," I purred to him erotically.

Dre grinned at the memory. "Hmmm ... yeah, that was the shit."

"That was nothing compared to what I got in mind for you tonight," I told him and gave him a kiss as my tongue played with his. Once again I gained the attention of some men watching as my dress rode up and exposed my red thong. We decided to get up and hit the dance floor. The DJ put on Mario's "Music For Love" and I let the baseline hit me. I started putting it on Dre like I was his personal stripper. Well, actually I was. I bent over and gyrated my ass on his crotch. Once again, all eyes were on me as niggas and some chicks were taking notes. After a few more songs, and a few more shots of Patron, we went and sat back down on the bed.

"Baby, I gotta go to the ladies room."

"Aight baby, hurry back."

"You know I will," I replied as I walked away. I had

to pee really bad. I guess the Patron ran right through me. Must be the reason I was so horny! After I came out of the ladies' room I saw a dude who was watching me on the dance floor.

I knew what he had in mind and I tried to avoid him but homie was on a mission.

"Hey momma, where you going," he said to me. "I got what you need right here baby girl." He smiled and showed me his fucked up yellow teeth. The muthafucka looked like Eddie Griffin on crack!

"Back to my man," I confirmed to him walking away but the nigga had the nerve to grab my arm. It looked like I was gonna have to bust a nigga head.

"Why you running away? I seen the way you were grinding on that nigga and I just wanna holla."

I snatched my arm away from him.

"Don't you ever put ya hands on me! What the fuck is wrong with you?"

He grinned and held his hands up in surrender. "No disrespect, I just think you can do better."

"Negro please, you better be glad my man ain't see you touch me or you'll be fucked up right now!" I turned to walk away.

"Drunk ass stripper bitch!"

Now why did he have to say that shit to me of all people? I stopped then turned back around and glared at him.

"You know what your problem is?" I said, walking back up on him. "You a weak ass nigga. Learn how to talk to a woman. Weak ass rap ... and fix ya mutherfucking grill before you try to talk to a chick. With them yellow, rotten teeth!" I yelled and walked away.

Walking back to the bed where Dre and I had been

sitting, I spotted him and he was getting his drink on. "Hey baby I'm ready to go."

"Already? You sure? We just got here." Dre looked at me, confused.

"Yeah, I'm sure."

"Something wrong?

"No, I just wanna go back to the hotel now."

"Aight, let's go." Dre got up off the bed and we left the club. I didn't tell him about what happened because I didn't want him to kill that fool. Plus I was already pissed off and needed to calm down. I was having a good time with my man and that bitch ass nigga had to bring me down. We drove back to the hotel and when we were back in our room, I went out onto the balcony to get some fresh air and gazed out onto the ocean. The view was beautiful at night. I shouldn't have let that nigga get to me when I was in such a beautiful city with my man.

"Hey baby? You okay," Dre asked.

I turned and looked at him. "Yeah. I'm sorry I was short with you at the club."

"Don't worry about it. I needed to talk to you alone anyway."

"What about?"

"Have a seat," Dre told me as he gestured toward the lounge chair on the balcony. I sat down and he stood in front of me.

"Nikki, for the past three years we've been kickin' it and I've never been this happy. We've been through hell and back and we're still here. You gave me a son, a little me. You're my lady … you've always been the one."

My heart was racing hearing him say what I think he was about to ask me. "What are you saying Dre?"

"What I'm trying to say ... I know we've talked about getting married after we had Tyler. In my mind you're already my wife but I just wanna make it official." Dre got down on one knee in front of me and took out a little black box. I couldn't believe this was finally happening. "You mean everything to me and I wanna give you the world. Nicole Bell, will you marry me?" Dre opened the box and I saw the biggest diamond I've ever seen sitting perfectly on top of a platinum band. I was speechless and just stared at the ring. "Nikki ... um, this is the part where you're supposed to say something?"

"What? Oh, yes! Oh god yes," I shouted excitedly as Dre smiled from ear to ear. He then slid the ring on my finger and my eyes began to water. I kissed Dre's lips. This was the most perfect moment of my life. I never thought I would ever be engaged to anyone, let alone, him. After stripping for six years I just thought that marriage wasn't meant for woman like me.

As we kissed, all those hurt feelings I had went away and the horny mistress in me came back out. Dre's tongue danced with mine and I felt my pussy get wet. He kissed my neck and shoulders as he slid one of my spaghetti straps off my shoulder, then the other, exposing my titties. My nipples were stiff as Dre sucked on them.

"Let's go back inside baby," Dre suggested to me but I had a better idea.

"No, let's do it right here," I hummed with a naughty grin on my face.

"What, you serious?" He looked around to see if anyone could see us.

"Uh huh," I replied as I sat down on the lounge chair and opened my legs for him. Dre slid his hands up my inner thighs and massaged them. My pussy was pulsating with excitement as I felt myself become wetter with each caress. Dre pulled my thong to the side and rubbed his thumb up and down my clit using my wetness to lube me up. Then he took his thumb and licked it clean.

"Just as sweet as ever," he said and pulled my thong down.

The cool sea breeze on the hot summer night made me feel even hornier as Dre licked my walls. I leaned back into the chair and bit my bottom lip as I felt his saliva mix with my wetness. When Dre pulled my ass to the edge of the chair, his tongue flicked my clit back and forth bringing my orgasm closer to the edge. I rotated my hips up and down as my pussy throbbed and that was when Dre unleashed his "Tasmanian Devil Tongue" on my pussy.

"Oh fuck! AAAAhhhh," I shouted at the top of my lungs not caring who heard me. Dre's tongue swirled around my clit as he slurped my juices up. My legs trembled uncontrollably as I climaxed. "Ah, ah, Dre! Please …"

Dre pulled back wearing my juices on his face and smiled. I stared in his eyes and smiled back as my orgasm rushed over me. No words were needed as I tried to catch my breath. Dre took off his Avirex polo revealing his muscular, sculpted chest. He stood up, unbuckled his belt and pulled down his pants. After he stepped out of his underwear, his elephant trunk dick stood out like a pole. Just looking at his body made me wet all over again. My pussy was still throbbing from his tongue-lashing.

"Stand up, turn around and face the ocean," Dre commanded.

I obeyed and put my hands on the balcony handrail, bent over and pushed my ass out. Dre stood behind me and smacked his hard dick against my ass.

"Oooh, you so hard," I turned and hummed to him.

"And your ass is so soft." Dre took the head of his dick and rubbed it up and down my pussy. Then he slowly pushed his shaft in me, inch by inch.

"Aahh ..." I moaned as he slowly stroked me from the back. Dre knew how to work me, slow and deep, making me feel every inch of his stiffness. I threw it back on him tightening my pussy to grip his dick when he pushed into me. There I was on the sixth floor of a hotel balcony with my dress around my waist and my titties hanging out getting hit doggy style by my fiancé. My pussy was jumping as I felt his manhood stroke me. I felt my pussy cum on his dick.

"Damnit Dre ... I love the way you fuck me," I said out of breath while he proceeded to hit me harder and faster gripping my hips. My pussy began to make a squishing sound as I begin to moan at the top of my lungs; my hands held tightly onto the railing as Dre pounded away. "Ah! Ah! Oh God!"

I looked out at the beach and saw passers-by looking up in our direction in search of our performance. They were too far away but it was too dark for them to really see us anyway. Besides I didn't mind being a hoe for Dre because soon I would be his wife. Dre withdrew out of me and my legs wobbled as I held onto the railing for balance.

"Let's go to the bed baby." He stood and waited for me to move. His dick was glistening in the moonlight, dripping with my cum.

"That sounds good but I can't walk baby."

Dre smirked. "Well, you don't have to." He walked over to me, picked me up and I wrapped my legs around his waist. Putting his hand under my ass for leverage, he took his hard dick and plunged it back into me. Dre pumped me deeply, kissing my lips as he walked us back into our room and laid me on the bed, careful not to take himself out of me. Then I let my legs spread further apart as he positioned himself on top of me and made love to me. He made love to me for hours before emptying himself inside me. My orgasm lasted another ten minutes until my pussy finally calmed down.

After Dre was done having his way with me I curled up on my side of the bed and went to sleep. I was so drained—literally. Dre spooned up behind me and I knew everything was all good. There was nothing like a real man to make a woman feel so good, but after awhile I didn't feel him behind me. Instead, I heard Dre on the phone outside on the balcony. His voice was raised, arguing with someone, so I listened.

"I don't give a damn what you think nigga! I paid you back every dime I owed you." He paused, and then yelled again. "No! What you need to do is stop calling my mutherfucking phone nigga! I don't owe you shit anymore … whatever nigga! It's like that? Well, suck my dick!" Dre became quiet and I knew he ended his call. He was irate and I knew in my heart that whatever was going on was going to be a major problem for both of us. I sat up in bed and waited for him to return. Moments later, Dre walked back into the room and looked at me. We shared an awkward silence.

Dre sighed, "You heard everything?"

"Yeah, what's going on?"

"I didn't want you to worry about this shit," he said

regrettably.

"Dre, if I'm going to be your wife then you have to be honest with me or this will never work. Are you hustling again?"

"No, I haven't been hustling for over three years now."

"Then what's going on? Who do you owe money to?"

"I don't owe money to nobody. Not anymore," Dre clarified.

"Well, what was that about?"

He hesitated briefly, then began speaking. "Back when I got arrested the police seized all of my supply and I owed my supplier a lot of money."

"How much money?"

"A little over $200,000, but for the last two years I've been paying him back every week from the profit we've made from the store."

I frowned. "Why didn't you tell me this before?"

"Because, it was my problem, you were having a baby and it was something I had under control."

"And now? What's changed?"

"This nigga Malachi said that I owe him interest and wants me to pay him another $100,000. What kind of bullshit interest rate is that?"

"Who's Malachi?"

"Malachi Turner. He was the nigga who was supplying me from Decatur. He has a connection to a drug lord in Colombia. This nigga is starting to take over most of Atlanta, becoming the number one dope supplier but he is trying to extort me and I ain't gonna let nobody do that," Dre explained and sat next to me on the bed.

"So what are we gonna do?"

"I've been talking to my nigga Polo and he said he would see what he can do to get Malachi off my back."

"And if he can't?"

Dre stared at me. "Then I'ma have to do what I gotta do."

"What about Tyler, Dre? What about me? We need you baby ... I thought we left all this bullshit behind us. I can't lose you now."

"Nikki, you ain't gonna lose me cause I ain't going nowhere. You're going to be my wife and I'm going to make sure we straight for life," Dre affirmed and caressed my face. "Come on, let's go back to bed."

Dre got back into bed with me and held me close but I just knew that the shit with Malachi wasn't going to be as easy to handle as Dre said it would. Why was this happening now? I just wanna be happy with Dre and Tyler so why can't I have that?

♛ ♛ ♛ ♛ ♛ ♛ ♛ ♛ ♛ ♛ ♛ ♛ ♛ ♛ ♛

Two weeks had passed since we left Miami and life was back to normal. I started to make plans for our wedding and we set a date for four months from now. I decided to hire a wedding planner instead of driving myself mad trying to arrange everything. I was at the shop working with Penny when Janelle came by to visit me.

I was so proud of my little cousin Janelle. She graduated from Georgia State University, got married to Jayson, and is now a Production Assistant working at Radio One, Hot 107.9. She didn't let her past as a stripper define her life. She was still so beautiful, even dressed casually in a pair of Deréon jeans and a pink Deréon hoodie and Air Force Ones.

"Girl I'm so excited about your wedding. When are you gonna pick out your dress?" Janelle demanded to know.

"Dress? I'm still trying to figure out what type of food I want at the reception!"

"Why are you worried? What's the point of hiring a wedding planner if you're gonna be stressed?"

"I don't know, I guess I'm just nervous."

"You don't got anything to be nervous about. You and Dre are going to happy together for years," Penny chimed in.

"I know … it just seems too good to be true."

"Is there something wrong Nikki?" Janelle queried, sensing there was something else on my mind.

"No, I'm fine. I just want everything to be perfect like you are with Jayson."

"Jayson and I are far from perfect but he's a wonderful man. We make it work. And now he's ready for us to start having kids."

"Are you ready?" Penny asked. "Cause I just got one and Tarius is a handful."

"Tarius done been here before with his little bad ass self! He's gonna be getting Tyler in all sorts of trouble when they get older." We all laughed then I looked at my cousin. "But J, are you ready for kids?"

"I am," she replied apprehensively.

"But?" I asked, sensing there was something she wasn't saying.

"It's just that I have a good chance of moving up quickly at my job and I don't know if I can have a baby now and still move ahead," Janelle said truthfully.

"Janelle, I know you can do anything you put your mind to. Don't let a job stop you and Jayson from starting a family if that's what you really want. Remember, we're here for you too."

"Thank you Nikki," Janelle replied and hugged me. We continued to talk about our lives and my wedding plans for the next few minutes when Dre walked into the store with Tyler. Tyler was two and a half years old and was a daddy's boy already. He loved Dre so much, sometimes he'd cry just because he knew he'd pick him up.

"Hey y'all," Dre acknowledged.

"What's up Dre," Janelle replied and went over to pick up Tyler. She loved him as if he were her son too. "Hey big man! How you doing," Janelle cooed to Tyler and kissed his chubby cheeks. Tyler loves to be kissed, especially from Janelle. He's going to be a little playa when he grows up.

"What y'all up to?" Dre asked and gave me a kiss.

"Nothing, just having girl talk."

He smirked. "Y'all talking about sex huh? That's all y'all women do."

"No, that's not all we do. You just nasty," Penny said to him.

"I know you know I'm nasty. I bet Nikki be giving y'all details blow by blow," Dre said braggingly.

"Shut up boy! I don't be talking about your narrow ass," I lied, not letting him know that we do talk about sex but it's only done at lunch when we have a drink or two. "We were talking about our wedding."

"Yeah Dre, you better enjoy your last few months of freedom. Anyway, I gotta get going. I'll call y'all later." Janelle kissed Tyler and gave him to me.

"Alright girl later." Janelle walked out of the store.

"You ready to go too Nikki?" Dre asked.

"Yeah." I turned to look at Penny. "Will you be alright here by yourself?"

"Girl I'll be fine," Penny confirmed. Dre, Tyler and I went outside to Dre's black Cutlass Deville. I swear he loved that car almost as much as me. A-Town Grillz was on the corner of Spring Street and Mitchell in the small business area of Midtown Atlanta. I put Tyler in his car seat in the back and got in on the passenger side.

"Damn," I exclaimed when I realized something was missing. "Dre I forgot Tyler's bag. It's behind the counter inside."

"Don't worry I'll get it." Dre got out and went back inside the store.

When he walked out of the store with the bag that's when everything started to move in slow motion for me. A white Crown Victoria with two people inside screeched out in front of Dre. He dropped the bag and started to in the opposite direction. Then I heard gunshots ring out.

"Dre!" I screamed as he collapsed on the sidewalk. The white car sped off down Spring Street. I got out of the car and ran toward Dre lying on his stomach and I saw a gunshot wound in his back. At that point I was freaking out. I got down on the ground and held Dre in my arms.

"Help me! Please somebody HELP ME!" I screamed at the top of my lungs. Penny came out of the store and ran over to me.

"Oh God … Nikki!" she yelled crying.

"Call the paramedics!"

"Okay!" Penny dialed on her cell phone. A few people on the street stoped and stared at me on the ground with Dre.

"Dre, Dre … baby please wake up," I plead with him but his eyes wouldn't open. "Please don't leave me … please …" I could feel the blood coming from Dre's body on me. Then I heard Tyler crying from inside the car. Penny ran over to the car to comfort him. My worst fear had come to life. The next few minutes was a blur as both cops and the paramedics crowded the area. The paramedics took Dre to Grady Memorial Hospital and Janelle drove me, following behind the ambulance. Tears rolled from my eyes as I sat in the waiting room and asked God, why? I was planning to have the wedding of my dreams and now I might have to plan a funeral for the man I loved more than anything else in the world. The police of course asked me what I saw and I told them what happened. I couldn't identify the two guys I saw in the car. The only thing I knew was that Dre had beef with Malachi Turner but I didn't tell the police that for some reason.

"Nikki I'm so sorry," Janelle said to me.

"What am I going to do now?" I asked feebly.

"It's going to be okay Nikki. Dre's a strong man he'll pull through this."

"We both are gonna be here for you and Tyler," Penny added.

I knew that they would be by my side but that still didn't change the fact that Dre was shot right in front of me and I knew whoever did it wasn't gonna stop until he was dead. Dre was in a coma. The doctors said he could wake up tomorrow or next year. It all depended on how fast his body could heal itself. I sat in his room holding his hand as tears rolled down my face. Not tears of sadness cause I already exhausted them but my tears were of anger. I was furious that Dre was shot down in the streets and there was nothing I could have done to stop it. I knew, Dre being an ex dope boy was reason enough for the cops to drag their feet on this case. Dre's friend, Polo, came to the hospital to see him and I knew he had to know who was behind his attempted murder for sure.

"Hey Polo," I greeted him as we stood by Dre's bed.

"Hey, Nikki … I know this is a hard time for you. I'm sorry this happened."

"I know, but you know who did this don't you?" I looked at him, trying to gauge his expression.

Polo shook his head, "Nikki …"

"You do! I know you do! Dre said some guy name Malachi Turner was trying to extort him."

"Nikki, you don't need to be talking about this now."

"Then when," I snapped in a raised tone. "He did this to Dre and you know it!"

Polo looked at me sadly. He was one of Dre's best friends.

"Yeah Malachi did it."

"Then what are you gonna do about it?"

He crinkled his eyebrows. "What you want me to do?"

"Kill him. That's what I want you to do," I coldly retorted.

Polo shook his head in disbelief. "Nikki, you don't know who Malachi is or just how powerful he is."

I turned and looked at Polo, not believing he said that to me. I put my left hand on my hip and pointed the index finger of my right hand in his face. "I don't give a fuck who he is! All I know is you're Dre's best friend and you're too much of a coward to kill the nigga that did this to him!"

Polo frowned because I called him out but I didn't give a fuck at this point.

"Nikki, Malachi is the biggest dope man in Atlanta. He ain't some corner boy. This nigga got an army around him. Ain't nobody stupid enough to try him."

I stared at him suspiciously. "He's supplying you too?"

"Yeah, he does. Listen Nikki, this nigga is so huge he even owns The Pink Palace. Nigga is paid," Polo explained to me.

"He owns The Pink Palace?" I said, shocked.

"You didn't know?" I shook my head. "I guess Dre ain't wanna tell you. Yeah he runs the place himself. I can't help you on this one Nikki. I'm sorry." Polo looked at Dre's unconscious body laying in the bed then walked away. It became clear to me that nobody was going to try Malachi. Not the police and definitely not Polo. But I couldn't just let go.

After Dre was stabilized, he was transferred to Emory and for the next three days, I was by his side, along with Tyler. Penny ran the store for me. I tried to move on but I couldn't. All I could think of was that this Malachi person did this to him. Sometimes I would just stare at Tyler and see Dre in him and cry. I felt like there was this hole in my chest and the only thing I could fill it with was rage.

Why was this happing to me? Why did this happen

to us? We were going to be a family. A real one? Dre was going to be my husband. Damn!

Chapter One

The Baddest Bitch

Atlanta, GA
Jacqueline "Jasmine" Dawson

The spotlight illuminated the long black runway-like stage. The smell of liquor and smoke lingered in the air throughout the dimly lit club. My skin tingled with excitement as my body glistened from the baby oil I rubbed all over. My breasts stood firm in my skimpy bikini top imprinting my erect nipples underneath. I stepped out on stage in my five hundred dollar red Prada shoes like a supermodel and gave the crowd of men ogling my curvy body my signature walk. It was more of a strut than a walk. Nobody could match my swagger as I grabbed the chrome pole and pulled my body upside down like a trained athlete. I wrapped my long, smooth, golden brown legs around pole and swung around until I touched the ground.

The crowd of horny men loved the way I flexed my body to the beat of Ray J's "Sexy Can I." I dropped into a split and made my ass clap as twenties and fifties flew like confetti on the stage. I stared into the eyes of this one dude, licked my full succulent lips and he was hypnotized. Without a word, I mentally commanded him to empty his wallet for me. When I took off my bikini top, it made him my slave. It was amazing how stupid men got when they saw titties. This one guy decided to make it rain and showered me with ones, tens, and a couple of twenties. I guess he thought all women were impressed by that when it was the dumbest thing I ever saw! You think a woman would throw money on the ground for a nigga? Dumbass!

I had been dancing at The Pink Palace for only ten months and I was already the top dollar bitch in the club. I made over a grand in less time than it took to fill out a job application. I walked out front and saw a new girl who called herself "Kandi." She did look sweet enough to lick alright. She was a young, tight thing, just like I liked.

I frowned up when I spotted her doing a table dance for the nasty little pervert, Reggie. He was Malachi's little brother and walked around the club like he owned the place. Half the time he'd be up in VIP trying to fuck with the girls or walking through the locker room like he was an inspector trying to look at everybody's ass for free. Nasty little troll was always scratching his crotch. That's why nobody with common sense and 20/20 vision would fuck with his ugly self. He may have been

Malachi's brother but he didn't have the money, power or respect his brother did.

I shook my head watching Kandi. Poor thing didn't know any better. Reggie was slapping her ass so hard I could hear it from where I was. She was smiling like she was enjoying it but I knew that shit had to sting. As I continued to look, I saw that he pulled her down into his lap and was rubbing all up on her. She was trying to stop him from digging his fingers underneath her thong bikini and looked toward the bouncer for help but he wasn't gonna say nothing to Malachi's little brother so I knew I'd better check the stupid nigga.

"Come on ... stop," Kandi said to him but he didn't.

"Damn you got a fatty, girl. Let me get a sniff." Reggie tried to lean his head forward.

"Reggie! Didn't you hear what she just said?" He stopped and smiled at me.

"Hey Jasmine, why don't you join us and let's get this shit really crunk!"

"How about I tell Malachi you're fucking with the girls again," I shot back at him and he glared at me.

"Get the fuck up," he spat to Kandi. She quickly did and started to walk away.

"Hold up. Don't leave so fast," I said to her and she looked at me confused but somewhat scared. "This nigga owes you for your lap dance."

"What? Bitch please!" Reggie rolled his eyes.

"Pay her ... now," I told him seriously. Reggie narrowed his eyes at me and angrily pulled out a wad of cash and peeled off a ten and handed it to her.

"Lap dances cost more than that," I informed him. He cut his eyes at me and then gave Kandi a twenty.

"Here. Now piss off!"

"Fuck you too," I snapped at him and took Kandi backstage with me.

"Thank you for helping me," Kandi said and smiled.

"No problem sweetie. Don't ever let me see you fucking with that dusty nigga again. Just because his brother owns this place don't make him shit." I turned my nose up in disgust remembering what he was doing to her.

"Okay," she replied shyly. She looked to be barely eighteen ... if that.

She resembled Rudi from "The Cosby Show" just sexier in a blue two-piece bikini and stilettos.

"You heading out?"

"Yeah, I'm done for the night and my feet are killing me," she grimaced as she shifted her weight from foot to foot. "Thank you Jasmine."

"Don't worry about. Just remember what I told you." I gave her a hug and seductively brushed a few stray hairs from her face. She smiled and then turned and walked toward the locker room backstage but then turned and looked back at me.

Gotcha.

Pretty young thing didn't know it yet but she was gonna be mine soon.

I looked around the club and noticed that there was nothing left but some small time niggas. I've already made my paper for the night so I might as well bounce too. Then I saw the man himself come through the club doors. Malachi Turner. Unlike his ugly ass brother Reggie, Malachi looked like money. Don't get me wrong Malachi was ugly too, but his money just made him a lot sexier.

Malachi was a big man, built like a linebacker. His shoulders were wide and his chest was solid so you know his $3,000 black Italian suit was tailor made to fit his hulk like frame. His hair was cut in a low Caesar fade with endless waves. His skin was a smooth jet-black complexion and his eyes were an intense dark brown. Rumor was that Malachi was "given" The Pink Palace by the previous owner and soon after nobody had seen him since. He intimidated even the hardest nigga that thought he was a thug. Fear in some ways was better than respect, although I didn't feel either when I was around him. The power of my pussy made him a different man behind closed doors. He strolled in with his niggas around him—his bodyguard, Big Bump and Ricky, one of his boys who ran the corners for him. His eyes scanned the room and when he saw me he gave me that lustful glare. He then made his way up the stairs to his office. It looked like I was gonna get some overtime tonight.

Malachi Turner

All eyes were on me as I walked into the club. Some looked at me with respect but most of them with fear. That was better. That made niggas easier to control. This was my club, my world, so that made me god. As I glanced across the club I saw that everything was running smoothly like a well-oiled stripper on a pole. The DJ was spinning a new track from Ludacris and there were two girls on stage shaking they ass like they supposed to. But then I saw my number one rump shaker standing at the bar looking finer than a bitch. Jasmine. Since she had been dancing here, business has been at an all time high. Just seeing her in that pink bikini made a nigga's dick rock hard.

But I had other things on my mind other than pussy. I spotted my idiot little brother, Reggie, fucking with some gals at a table. Stupid nigga thinks with his dick more than the goddamn sense he was born with. He better had taken care of the shit I told him to do. He saw me and straightened himself up. I headed upstairs to my office with Ricky behind me. Bump stood outside my door and Ricky took a seat in front of my mahogany desk. I walked to the window behind my chair and looked down at the club. I saw Reggie coming upstairs to see me.

"Do you think Reggie got that shit taken care of?" Ricky asked.

"He better had. Did you link up with Jorge?"

"Yeah, right on time as usual. Detective Raymond made sure we stayed off the radar."

Big Bump opened my door and let Reggie in.

"What's up bruh?" He turned and saw Ricky and scowled. He made no secret of his dislike of him. Reggie thought that just because he was my brother that he should be running the corners instead of Ricky. He was my brother but he's also a fuck up. Ricky handled whatever I tell him to do without screw-ups.

"You can't say hello Reggie?" Ricky said to him sarcastically.

"Rick," Reggie croaked dryly.

"Did you get that thing done Reggie?" I asked.

"Hell yeah. That nigga Dre ain't gonna be a problem for ya anymore."

"Good."

"I told ya I would handle that bitch. You should let me handle more shit for you bruh," Reggie bragged and looked at Ricky who only smiled and shook his head. "You got something to say to me Ricky?"

"If I got something to say to you nigga then I'll say it," Ricky informed with a lot more bass in his voice, still sitting in the chair, not letting Reggie shake him. "Look at this nigga … Just because you took care of some small time nigga for Malachi you think you can do what I do? You silly nigga," Ricky laughed.

"Fuck you Rick! Dre was one of the biggest dealers in Atlanta and I handled that nigga! Keep on talking shit and I'll handle yo bitch ass too!"

Ricky stood up and got in Reggie's face. I knew if Reggie wasn't my brother Ricky would've put a bullet in his head by now. He had killed niggas for much less in the streets. "You can't handle shit nigga. That's why Malachi keeps your bitch ass up in this club where he can watch yo baby ass." Ricky was correct in his assessment. Reggie was too immature to be left on his own in the streets. I promised our mother I would take care of his ass before she passed away. But with Reggie killing Dre for me he was starting prove himself.

"Both of you shut ya bloodclot mouth." I took a seat behind my desk and pulled out an already rolled spliff from my top drawer. "You did good Reggie. Just do as I tell you and I'll give more shit to do in the future." My private line started to ring and I looked at the caller ID. "Both of y'all get da fuck out. I gotta take dis call."

They both walked out of my office and I picked up the phone. "Hello?"

"Hey Daddy," my six-year-old daughter Courtney

screeched happily.

"What are you doing up so late?"

"I couldn't sleep, Daddy. Mommy said it would be alright if I called you. When are you coming by?"

That whore of a mother of hers knew I wouldn't be back over in Dunwoody until this weekend. She does this shit on purpose to tess me. She knew Courtney was the only way she could see me on a regular basis. "Baby girl, Daddy has a lot of work to do, so I won't make it over there until later."

"Okay," she replied sadly.

"But no worries sweetheart, when I see you I'm gonna have a surprise for you."

"Really?" Her mood was beginning to pick up.

"Yes, really. Now go to bed and I'll call you in the morning."

"Okay Daddy."

"I love you, Courtney."

"I love you too, Daddy."

"Okay now put ya mother on the phone." I looked down through the window and spotted Jasmine sitting at the bar looking up at me. I gestured for her to come up as I heard Courtney giving the phone to her mother, Latoya.

"Yeah," she said dryly.

"What did I tell yuh about putting shit in Courtney's head," I growled at her.

"I just told her if she wants to see her daddy then call him," Latoya snapped with attitude.

"Yuh gonna stop romping wit mi, Latoya! You gonna stop dat shit or ..."

"Or what nigga? I'm the mother of yo child! You should be here with us instead of that damn club fucking wit them strippers!"

"Don't forget that I met yo ass in a strip club shaking yo ass too bitch! And if yuh wanna keep living in that big fuckin' house that I'm paying for yuh, do what the fuck I tell yuh to," I remind her. Silence fell across the line as she thought about what I just told her. Big Bump opened my door and let Jasmine in.

"I just want us to be a family again Malachi … you know I love you."

Jasmine walked over and sat her sexy, fat, round ass on my desk.

"Yuh just remember what I said and there won't be any problems," I told her and hung up. Jasmine spun her fat ass around on my desk and faced me.

"Wifey stressing you out?" she laughed.

"She's not my bumbaclot wife."

"I hate seeing you so upset Malachi."

Jasmine kicked off her shoes then seductively rubbed her feet up my slacks and found my rock hard dick. She was so fucking sexy. I grabbed one of her long thick legs. Her calves were muscularly sculpted from hours of dancing.

"What you got for me baby?" she asked.

I pulled six Ben Franklins from my pocket and dropped it on my desk. She skillfully scooped them up and tucked them underneath her pink bikini top. Then she dropped in between my legs and unzipped my slacks. After she pulled out my massive dick she darted her tongue around the tip then licked my sensitive spot just below head. That shit sent shivers up and down my shaft. Her technique was the shit. I leaned back in my chair and she deep throated me and milked my dick for the next hour. She served me like everybody else. Like

I said this was my world and I am god.

Chapter Two

Paranoia

Atlanta, GA
Nikki

As much as I hated to leave Dre's side I had to get back to Penny at the shop. Between Penny and Janelle coming in helping her out, business was still coming into the store and bills needed to be paid. It had been one week since Dre was hospitalized and I had already received two bills. I knew there were more to come because we didn't have health insurance. I was lucky Dre and I had some paper saved away for Tyler's college fund. I hated to touch it but I didn't have much choice.

What the hell am I gonna do now? I thought as I rode down the elevator in Emory hospital. How can I run the business, take care of Tyler and continue to pay Dre's medical expenses before we're completely broke? I was glad Obama got the health care plan past them fools in Washington.

I walked through the walkway from the lobby to the parking garage and took another elevator to the fourth level. As I walked to Dre's black Cutlass Deville I heard somebody bumping T.I.'s Paper Trail album. I looked down the garage and saw a black Escalade on 24-inch rims. The windows were a dark tint so I couldn't see who was inside. I got a bad vibe for some reason but still got in the Cutlass and started it up. I pulled out of the parking space and drove by the Escalade. Nothing happened. Maybe I was still a little paranoid.

👑 👑 👑 👑 👑 👑 👑 👑 👑 👑 👑 👑 👑 👑 👑 👑

I got to the shop and saw Penny and Janelle holding down the fort for me. They didn't know how much I loved them for stepping in and helping me the way they did. Penny was checking a lady out at the counter and Janelle walked over to me and gave me a hug.

"What's up cuz?" Janelle asked. She was at the display table folding jeans while Penny was running the register.

I sighed, "Same old shit."

"No change in Dre?"

"No. The doctors are still telling me they don't know when he could come out of this."

"I'm so sorry Nikki," Janelle said to me sincerely.

"You don't need to be. That muthafucka Malachi is the one who is gonna be sorry."

Janelle stopped folding the jeans in front of her.

"Malachi? Who's that?" Janelle queried.

I shouldn't have let his name come out of my mouth.

"Is he the one that did this to Dre?"

I sighed and walked behind the counter. "Yes."

Janelle stepped to the counter and stared at me. "Why didn't you tell the police?"

"I don't have any proof he did it. Plus I don't trust them fuckin' cops either." Shit. I shouldn't have said that knowing that her husband Jayson is a cop too. "I'm sorry Janelle. I know Jayson is a good man."

"It's okay Nikki. Who is this Malachi?"

"He's the new owner of The Pink Palace," I revealed to her and Janelle shook her head. It seemed like a lifetime ago we both used to dance up in there. Janelle has done her best to put that place behind her and here I was bringing it back up. "He and Dre did some business together back when he was hustling. When Dre got busted he still owed him some money. For the last three years Dre has been paying him back, and after he paid him what he owed, Malachi wanted to extort more money from him."

"Let me guess … Dre refused to give him any more money and Malachi went after him," Janelle deduced as she came around the counter.

"Yeah. Piece of shit couldn't just let him be. He just took him … from me," I said as tears watered my eyes.

"It's okay Nikki," she patted my back. "We'll get through this together. Maybe I can ask Jayson to look into this Malachi and see what he can turn up."

"No. Janelle." I grabbed her hand and looked at her seriously. "I got you involved with Damien's psycho ass and he almost raped you. I'm not gonna get you twisted up with this nigga too. This is not your problem."

"Nikki, I'm a big girl now and I know what you went through with Damien. I won't let you go through it again with anybody else." Janelle still thought it was her fault that Damien and Horse nearly raped and beat me to death three years ago. It was my own reckless lifestyle that put me in that situation in the first place. I wouldn't put Janelle in harm's way again.

"Don't worry Janelle I'll be fine. Just don't tell Jayson about this. Malachi will get what he's got coming sooner or later. They always do. For now my only concern is Dre's health and raising Tyler. I just don't want him to grow up without his father."

"He's gonna pull out of this Nikki. I know it."

I wished I could have been as sure of that as Janelle was. It's been over a week since Dre slipped into a coma and nobody knew anything. I had to be realistic about it. He may never wake up. God … you can't do this to us. We've gone through so much already. We both changed so much just to have our past come and bite us in the ass. Please God just help my family, I prayed.

♔ ♔ ♔ ♔ ♔ ♔ ♔ ♔ ♔ ♔ ♔ ♔ ♔ ♔ ♔ ♔

The next morning I dropped Tyler off at the daycare and headed to the hospital. As I drove down Peachtree Street past the Fox Theater I spotted a black Escalade two cars behind me. A chill went up my spine. I thought it was the same Escalade I saw in the parking garage of the hospital yesterday. Was it following me? I knew I wasn't being paranoid now. Who is it? Is it Malachi? Is he keeping tabs on me? Or is he trying to finish the job he started and kill Dre?

I quickly pulled my car into a parking lot and the Escalade drove by. I looked through my rearview mirror and saw a guy behind the wheel. Same 24-inch rims I saw yesterday. The tinted windows were down and I got a real good look at his face. Never saw him before but I knew a dope boy when I saw one. He must work for Malachi. He wasn't going to let this go until Dre was dead. What am I gonna do now?

Jasmine

Some folks might call me materialistic, money hungry or superficial and you know what? They're absolutely right! Fuck a dollar and dream! I need hundred dollar bills to make me cream! I got The Pink Palace on lock. Plus I got Malachi breaking me off extra for the exclusive favors I give him. With Malachi giving me top billing I can afford to live the lavish life in this luxury condo in Buckhead. Furnished with top of the line Italian furniture, contemporary appliances and fixtures, including a washer and dryer. Not to mention a private indoor pool and private parking lot.

Like I said before, I wasn't an average stripper shaking my ass at a hole in wall club. I wasn't just another black girl lost from a broken home with daddy issues. As a matter of fact, I grew up with both of my parents in the house and I graduated from Spelman College with a Bachelors degree in economics. I started dancing at the Red Light Club to help me pay tuition. After finishing school and seeing how much money I was making a night from dancing I decided not to take an internship getting coffee for some jackass in a suit.

But what sets me apart from the average chick in the club was more than my pretty face, big titties, bubbly personality and my voluptuous ass. It was my ambition. I never got caught up in the stripper lifestyle. This was a business and I'm all about my business. I have my own website, Myspace page, Facebook, and Twitter. I have over 25,000 followers on Twitter and Facebook where I sell my own calendar with photos I had taken by Marion Designs in Atlanta. I also do private parties and travel around the country to other clubs to dance for the right price. Everywhere from Magic City, Sues Rendezvous, The Rollexxx Club, and Erotic City. I get money!

I got no regrets ... well, as far as my career choice. None. But I wished I never lost the friendship of my girls Rashida and Joyce. Especially Rashida. I loved her. Let's just say things ended badly. I still got the lumps to prove it. But fuck it, that's the past. Money over niggas and bitches is my creed now and as long as I have Malachi's nose wide open, my cash flow is unlimited.

♛ ♛ ♛ ♛ ♛ ♛ ♛ ♛ ♛ ♛ ♛ ♛ ♛ ♛ ♛ ♛ ♛

I drove to the Pink Palace in my silver CLS550 Mercedes Benz and once I got inside I saw my new plaything, Kandi. She was in the locker room looking in the mirror putting on her makeup. She was a cutie pie with that satin lace flyaway babydoll. Her fat little camel toe was imprinted through her matching satin panties. Just looking at her made me wet.

"Hey Kandi," I said to her as I walked up behind her.

"Hey Jasmine," she replied in a perky tone.

"You getting ready to hit the stage?"

"Yeah, I hope I can make a little extra money tonight," she confirmed as she finished applying her pink MAC lipstick.

"How come?" I asked.

"I just got some bills I need to catch up on."

"Your boyfriend can't help you out?"

"He tries," Kandi said, then turned around and stared at me. "But he's a college student too. He ain't crazy about me working here either."

"What's going on?"

"He thinks I'm fucking every nigga in the club." She shook her head at the recollection. "He's so stupid. This is just a job."

"I hear ya. Men can be so damn insecure," I cosigned and caressed her arm. I could tell she didn't mind my touch. That was always a good sign. "Listen, if you wanna make a little extra cash I can hook you up."

"Really?"

"Yeah, I do a few private shows around town and I can take you with me. The money is good and the niggas are usually corporate types. Pushovers. Show 'em a little ass, let 'em touch a titty and you'll get paid. If you up for it just let me know."

"Am I? Hell yeah! I'm trying to get this money. Good looking out Jasmine." She hugged me. "Ya'know, at first I was a little nervous here not knowing anybody but you really be looking out for me. Thank you."

"It ain't nothing but a thing. I'll let you know when my next gig is."

"Cool, I better get on stage now. Talk to you later."

I watched as Kandi walked to the stage. Oh sweet Kandi, I'ma gonna take very good care of you alright.

I turned, looked in the mirror and smiled. I walked to the side of the stage and watched Kandi on stage doing her thing on the pole. The way she did them splits, I couldn't wait to get in between them thighs.

As I watched the show I saw a sexy ass chocolate sista walk up in the club. Seeing a chick up in the club was nothing new. They're some of my best tippers. She was rockin' a V-neck blue Versace blouse, Seven Jeans that look like they were painted on that fat ass and black Steve Madden stilettos. But this chick wasn't here for the show. She made her way to the stairs leading to Malachi's office. No way the security was gonna let her up to Malachi's office no matter how good she looked. What the fuck? They just let her go up. That's not Malachi's wife … who is she?

Chapter Three

Dining With the Devil

Atlanta, GA
Malachi

"I checked up on that job you had Reggie do," Ricky said as he sat in front of me. Ricky had been my right hand man for about ten years now and he's my most reliable soldier in the game.

"And?"

"Well, I found out that nigga Dre is up in Emory in a coma."

I frowned. "A coma?"

"Yep. Looks like Reggie didn't quite get the job done like he thought," Ricky quipped as he sat casually, checking his iPhone.

"Damn. I swear that nigga can't piss straight without making a mess," I grumbled as I looked out of the window at Reggie sitting at a table getting a dance from a girl. As I was looking at my retarded little brother I noticed the most stunning woman I had seen in a while walk in the club. I saw ass everyday and I could fuck any bitch in here I wanted so I wasn't easily impressed with too many women but this one got my attention immediately. She walked through the club with confidence and seemed to have a glow about her. She was flawless.

"Who is dat?" I asked Ricky. He stood up and looked at her through the window.

"That's the chick I been following around in Dre's car. I think that's his girl. She's heading straight up here. Do you want me to tell security to keep her there?"

"No. Let her come up."

Damn she looked good. No wonder Dre decided to get out of the game. If she's brave enough to come here then the least I could do was meet her. Ricky made a call to security and they let her up. When I saw her, she was even more breathtaking up close. The look in her eyes though was of distain for me. For some reason that aroused me even more. She cut her eyes to Ricky as if telling him she knew he was following her. Then she refocused her eyes on me. If security hadn't patted her down she maybe would have brought a gun up here to kill me. Most people show fear around me but not her. She came straight to my desk and stared me in my eyes.

"You wanted to see me?" I asked as I leaned back in my chair and looked at her lovely body in before me. Her thickness in them jeans was astonishing.

"Malachi Turner," she said in a smooth even tone. "I

believe we have a mutual acquaintance common."

"That might be so but who may I ask are you?"

"My name is Nikki Bell. You've done business with my baby's father Andre Wade," she said proudly.

Hmmm … not too many women would walk into the lion's den for a nigga like his.

"What can I do for you Ms. Bell?"

"I need for you to leave him alone. He's no threat to you or your business."

I smiled at the beautiful woman brave enough to speak to me so boldly. "Dre was never a threat to my business but there was a matter of a debt he owed me."

"A debt he had paid in full," she snapped.

"His debt isn't paid until I say it is," I coldly told her.

She exhaled deeply and then glanced at Ricky who was eyeing her like a shark. If looks could kill Ricky would've been done.

"Then I wanna know what I need to give you in order to settle it."

No fear. I've rarely come across a woman with this kind of determination since I left Kingston years ago. She intrigued me. "Ricky, give us a moment alone."

Ricky nodded at me and then gave Nikki another lustful glare before he left the room. "Have a seat."

"I'd rather stand," she insisted but there was only so much willfulness I would allow in my world. I am god here.

"I said sit," I commanded in a more powerful tone. She reluctantly obeyed. I got up and walked around my desk and stood in front of her. Her luscious breasts rose and fell with each deep breath she took. The look on her face was steadied, still no fear. "What can you give me that I don't already have, Nikki?"

"What do you want? I can give you money but you don't look like a man who needs the few dollars I can give you. Dre is the father of my son. I don't want him to grow up without his father in his life. As a man, I'm sure you can understand what that can do to a boy," she said sincerely. "That's all he has. Don't take that away from him. Please?"

No one has ever appealed to me in this fashion. A woman like her is who I can see with a nigga like me with. I could fuck her but she would never really give herself to me … not at first. No, a woman like her must be broken before she will give in. Materialistic things don't seem to move her like most of these bitches in here. Most women would come in here with their pussy in my face but not her.

"He's in a coma. He might be with Jah soon. No telling if he will ever wake up … if he's allowed to at all.

"Don't take him away from us."

I watched her plea for Dre and placed my hands behind my head. "Perhaps we can come to some kind of agreement. Maybe we can discuss this further over a nice meal?"

She looked at me inquisitively as if weighing her options. "A meal? With me?"

"Yes dinner. You do eat?" I could tell she expected me to ask her for something else.

"Yes of course. When?"

"Tomorrow night. I'll send a car for you, say … around eight?"

"What about Dre?"

"He'll be fine. We'll discuss his future as well," I

assured and extended my hand toward her. She stared at it then took it and she stood. I kissed her hand and a sweet smell of cherries filled my nostrils. My dick started to rise in my boxers and she gently pulled her hand away.

"That's fine," she told me then turned and walked to the door. Her ample ass bounced with every step. My dick wanted her ass right now. She opened the door but before she left, she turned and looked at me one last time before exiting my office. A few seconds passed and Ricky came back inside.

"Damn Malachi, I know what you're gonna do with all that ass right there."

"My yute, I want you to keep tabs on her. I wanna know her every move. You can never be too sure what a woman can be up to."

"Consider it done," Ricky said and left my office. I knew exactly what she had in mind. It's been a long time since I had a challenge walk through my doors.

Nikki

That was the scariest Jamaican I had ever seen in my life. My heart felt like it was about to jump out of my chest. I've dealt with his type before so I know how to handle myself around him. I didn't tell Janelle or Penny I was going to do this cause I knew they would try and stop me. But if I didn't do this I knew he'd kill Dre. His boy Ricky was the one following me around town. My gut told me he worked for Malachi.

Nothing much has changed since the last time I'd been up in the Palace. Mostly new girls but they all do the same old tricks on stage. Same horny ass men up in there, a few of them I know from my days of work there. They stared at me like I was brand new. Guess they're not used to seeing me with my clothes on. As I walked through the club I spotted this one girl staring at me from the bar. She must've thought I was here to audition for a job. Bitch please!

I was prepared to do anything to convince Malachi not to hurt Dre. I knew that sex would most likely be my only option but he surprised me. He wanted to take me out to dinner. He must wanna get a full stomach before we fuck. Whatever, as long as he left Dre alone I was willing to do whatever he wanted. Once I stepped out of the club I got to my car and took off. I turned down Spring Street and entered I-75/I-85 and headed toward College Park.

👑 👑 👑 👑 👑 👑 👑 👑 👑 👑 👑 👑 👑 👑 👑 👑

The next day I was at the shop with Penny. I still replayed last night's events in my head, trying to figure if there was something else I could've done. Penny was putting some clothes back on the rack as I sat behind the counter in deep thought.

"What are you thinking about?" Penny asked me as she put the Averix hoodies on display.

"Nothing."

"Nikki, you can't keep worrying about Dre. I know it's hard not to but you can't dwell on it every second of the day."

"Penny," I sighed briefly. "I need to tell you something and it's gotta stay between us." Penny had been my girl for years. We've done all sorts of things together, from our time dancing at the Pink Palace, doing private shows for niggas, and even a few threesomes. There wasn't nothing that could shock her. In some ways she knew me better than anybody else so I knew she'd understand what I was going to tell her.

"You already know, what's up?"

"I went to the Pink Palace to see Malachi," I told her and she stopped and looked at me, disappointed.

"And why would you go and do something like that Nikki?" Penny said to me, upset.

"Because the other day when I was leaving the hospital I saw a dude in black Escalade watching me. Then yesterday the same Escalade was following me around town. Something told me it was Malachi trying to find out what condition Dre was in and when I went to club I saw the same nigga in Malachi's office with him."

"Oh my God ... what happened?"

"Malachi is a big scary ass Jamaican. Powerful, arrogant and a control freak. I just wanted to look him in the eye and see if I could reason with him. I needed to say something, anything to convince him to leave Dre alone."

"Nikki we both know niggas like Malachi only want one thing from women like us."

"I know. He had that look in his eye. I love Dre but if it meant fucking that nigga to get him to back off I was prepared to do that too," I said to her and Penny understood. We both knew that the power of pussy is the ultimate bargaining commodity that we have. Penny walked up to the counter in front of me.

"So what happens now?" she asked.

"He wants to take me out to dinner. Can you keep

Tyler for me tonight?"

"Yeah no problem. I know you have to do what you have to do Nikki but I don't wanna see you get hurt either. I don't think I could stand to see another man hurt you like that again," Penny admitted and took my hand. She stood by my side while I recovered from the abuse Damien put me through years ago.

"That's not going to happen to me again. I'm not playing games like that anymore. I got too much to lose this time around."

👑 👑 👑 👑 👑 👑 👑 👑 👑 👑 👑 👑 👑 👑 👑

I started getting dressed around 7:15 for my dinner date with Malachi. I couldn't believe I was about to break bread with the nigga responsible for putting Dre in a coma. Not to mention what else he may have had in mind for me. But it didn't matter; as long as Dre's life was at stake I was willing to do anything to protect him.

I decided to wear a simple black Dolce & Gabbana cocktail dress that showed plenty of legs, matching Prada heels and a silver necklace with a heart shaped pendant. My hair was in an updo with two Chinese hair sticks in the back. My MAC makeup was flawless as I gave myself a once over in the mirror.

Eight o'clock sharp a black stretch limo pulled up in front of my house. Funny how Malachi knew where I lived already. Once I walked outside, the driver got out and opened my door for me. Malachi was trying to impress me. Pretty soon we drove down Old National Highway and got on I-85 north to Midtown Atlanta. My only thought was what did I have to do to get Malachi to leave Dre alone?

The driver exited off of 249-B, then turned down Peachtree Street and we soon pulled in front of The Melting Pot fondue restaurant. The driver let me out and I walked to the door and went inside. It was a dimly lit restaurant that was sectioned off for a more intimate feel.

The hostess behind the podium smiled at me. "Hello, welcome to the Melting Pot. Do you have a reservation?"

"Yes, I think it's under the name Malachi Turner."

She looked over her guest book. "Yes, please come with me."

She escorted me through the restaurant and we passed by a glass wall with what looked like a hundred bottles of wine secured on it, then around the corner down a passageway past the bar. Then she turned another corner and led me to a booth in the back where I saw Malachi sitting at a table waiting for me. He stood up and smiled, as he looked me up and down.

"Hello Nikki," he said in a deep Jamaican accent. He was dressed to the nines in a custom tailored tan suit and brown gators. He exuded the same confidence he had the other night.

"Hello Malachi," I acknowledged as I took a seat.

"Your server will be with you in a moment," the hostess told us and walked away. I tried to calm my nerves as I looked at the menu.

"You look exquisite tonight Nikki."

"Thank you."

"I'm glad you decided to dine with me tonight."

"I didn't have much of a choice," I replied as I tried to hold back my discontent with the thought of eating with him.

"Of course you had a choice and you choose to be here with me tonight."

"Nice restaurant," I told him trying to change the subject.

"Yes, it's one of my favorite places to eat. I know you'll enjoy the cuisine."

To my surprise I did enjoy the fondue dipped shrimp and steak. I was surprised at how fast and delicious the meat was cooked in the small fondue pot on the oven-topped table in front of us. For the most part Malachi talked about himself like most egomaniacs. He enjoyed the sound of his own voice. He told me about leaving Jamaica when he was 15 years old and his rise to power in Atlanta. Surprisingly enough he bought the Pink Palace just a few months after I quit working there. I wondered if he knew I used to dance there. Then he flipped the conversation to me.

"So how old is your son?"

I paused for a moment, unsure if I wanted to talk about Tyler with him. "He'll be three in March."

"What's his name?"

"Tyler."

"Good name."

"Yes, his father gave him it," I told him and he smirked.

"I can see you're a woman very loyal to her man."

"That's the only reason I'm here."

"No it's not. There were a number of ways you could've handled this situation."

I put my fork down and glared at him. "You gave me no choice. You were going to kill Dre."

"I never said that to you. I just merely asked you out

to dinner."

"Then why did you have your boy Ricky following me around at the hospital?"

"I wanted to have an update on Dre's situation. If you thought I was going to harm him you could've gone to the police," Malachi said then took another bite of his steak.

As he ate, I wanted to grab his knife and stab him in the eyes for what he did to Dre.

"But you didn't. You choose to come to me. You choose to come to dinner with me tonight because I'm the type of nigga a woman like you wants."

Muthafucka. In some ways he was right. Back in the day I would've been all up on him doing whatever and taking his money but I wasn't that woman anymore. Not after what I'd been through.

"The only thing I want is for you to leave Dre alone. I'm here willing to do whatever it takes to make that happen. If sex is what you want then let's just get to that and stop all this wining and dining shit."

"Finish your food," Malachi said and continued to eat his as if he didn't hear me. Arrogant son of a bitch.

Chapter Four

Sexual Seduction

Buckhead, GA
Jasmine

"I'll come pick you up from the club around ten," I told Kandi over the phone.

"That'll be good. Thanks for hooking me up with this party Jasmine!"

"Like I said, it's no problem. Just be ready to make this money."

"I'm ready for whatever! See you in a few," Kandi replied and I hung up.

Hmmm, ready for whatever huh? We'll see young Kandi, we'll see. I looked myself over in the mirror. I was wearing a gray V-neck Elizabeth and James dread cardigan with a black lace bra underneath. The cardigan hung on my body like a mini-skirt showing off my long thick legs and I had on gray, python-printed Christian Louboutin pumps. I wore two silver Cuban link chains with a cross and a Hello Kitty charm on the other. My hair was down, parted in the middle looking good after my trip to Alres Salon and Spa and my makeup was flawless as usual. I was the shit!

I jumped in my silver CLS550 Mercedes Benz and headed to the Pink Palace. I decided to go through the city and down Peachtree Street. I was blasting Lil' Wayne's "Lollipop" as I cruised down the street. Sweet Kandi was definitely gonna be my lollipop tonight. As I got closer to the club I stopped at a red light and saw a limo outside of the Melting Pot restaurant and then I saw Malachi and the chick I saw at the club the other night come out. Who the hell was she? I had to admit that she looked cute in her black Dolce and Gabbana cocktail dress. Bitch got style, but how did she get so close to Malachi so quickly? Something was going on. The light changed to green and I pulled off and headed to the Pink Palace.

Once I got to the club, I saw Kandi standing out front waiting for me. She had on a white tube top and mini-skirt with black stilettos. I was going to have to step her fashion game up in the future. I pulled up to the curb and she opened the door and jumped in.

"Hey Jasmine! Girl I couldn't wait for you to get here."

"I see." I looked her up and down and lied, "Cute outfit you got on."

"This ain't nothing compared to what you got on. What did you do? Raid Rihanna's closet? That shit is hot!"

I looked down at what I had on. To me, it was no big deal. "I just threw this together. I'll hook you up with some stuff later if you'd like."

"Hell yeah! Jasmine you my girl! So where is this party at?" Kandi asked as I turned on to I-20 west.

"It's out in Lithonia. Some local rapper named Young Reezy wants me to entertain them tonight. You know how the young niggas with record deals spend cash."

"Yeah, he's got that song called Booty Butterfly. When you said entertain them you mean just dancing right?" Kandi asked nervously.

"I'ma be real with you Kandi, if you wanna get down with Young Reezy that's on you. Personally his paper ain't long enough for me to give him some pussy. We're just going there and do our thing and get paid alright?"

"That sounds good to me."

About 20 minutes later we pulled into a private neighborhood in Lithonia. There were about thirty cars parked in front of a big house, almost like a mini mansion. Kandi and I parked and walked up to the front door and rang the bell. Music was blasting from inside of the house. A few seconds later the door opened.

"Oh shit," a young nigga said, as he looked us up and down. He had on a long white tee, baggy black jeans, and a red A-town hat.

"We're tonight's entertainment," I told him and he let us in. The house was full of niggas with a few chicks here and there. I scanned the room and spotted Young Reezy sitting in the center of a long L-shaped sofa surrounded by groupies and his entourage. Young Reezy was iced out with four platinum chains, diamond-encrusted bracelets around each wrist and a diamond-encrusted grill in his mouth. I swear these rappers didn't know what to do with their money. He glanced over and smiled then nodded his head.

"Can you take us to a room so we can change?" I asked the young nigga who let us in. His eyes were glued on my ass.

"Uh yeah. Dis way," he told me and led us to a room down a long hallway. It had a big bed and a 42-inch plasma hanging on the wall that was hooked up to a PS3. The dresser had a bunch of games and a collection of porn on it. The boom-boom room no doubt. The dude that let us in was still standing at the door ogling us.

"Where's my money?"

He looked at me confused. "Huh?"

"Money nigga! We needs to get paid before anything pops off," I yelled as I looked him up and down.

"Yeah, I got ya," he grumbled as he went out to the party. I turned and looked at Kandi.

"Always get your money first. No cash, no ass."

"I know that's right," Kandi agreed as she sat on the bed. A few minutes later the dude came back with an envelope and gave it to me. I counted the cash. Ten thousand in hundred dollar bills as agreed. The dude was once again staring at us.

"You can leave now," I told him and closed the door in his face. I counted out three thousand and gave it to Kandi. "Here you go girl."

"Damn Young Reezy is ballin' huh?"

"Kandi, don't be sucked in by this. This ain't real money. This dude got a little paper. This is just some nigga spending all his advance money on bullshit. Trust me, if you stick with me I'll show you the niggas with cash." She nodded and then went into her bag and pulled out a bikini then started to undress. Her body was curvy and tight. Her ass was round and fat and I felt myself getting wet looking at her. Kandi turned and looked at me.

"Aren't you gonna change?"

"Yeah."

She had no idea. I pulled off my cardigan and noticed that she was looking at me. I looked up at her and grinned. She smiled back nervously and continued to get dressed. I changed into my black panties with the furry balls hanging from it and slipped on my black high heeled Prada shoes. A few minutes later we left the room and walked back out to the living room and all eyes were on us. Niggas were drooling and bitches were turning up their noses and hating, mad that they didn't look as good as us.

"Who's Young Reezy?" I yelled as if I don't know and he smiled.

"That's me!"

I gestured with my finger for him to come here and his niggas started to squeal and yell as I called him out. He got up and met me in the center of the room.

"So you the one that made that song 'Booty Butterfly'?"

"Yeah," he said and smiled.

"What you know about that?" I asked as I traced my fingers over his chest and down to his crotch.

"I know what I know."

"Well let me show you what a real booty butterfly is," I told him. Kandi took her cue and grabbed a chair and put it behind him. I pushed him back into it. "Play that shit!"

The DJ started the song, "Booty Butterfly, Booty

Butterfly, make ya ass cheeks flap like a butterfly/ Booty Butterfly, Booty Butterfly, make ya ass cheeks flap like a butterfly."

I bent over and started to make my ass clap in his face. Kandi joined me and the niggas went wild. Reezy started to smack our asses softly and I decided to give him a ride. I sat in his lap and gyrated my ass until I felt his hard dick through his jeans. Kandi started to dance for some other niggas and they started tipping her.

"Oh shit!" Young Reezy yelled.

I love exciting niggas.

"You like my butterfly?" I asked, rolling on him.

"Hell yeah, shit! I like both of y'alls butterfly!"

"You do? Kandi, Reezy likes your booty butterfly too," I yelled at her and she strutted over to us. She bent over and started to clap her ass for him while I continued to ride. I got up and then Kandi straddled him cowgirl style in the chair.

"Yeah!" Reezy yelled.

"Let's take this to the next level," I said and slid up behind Kandi. We were both on Reezy and then I slid my hand down Kandi's stomach and underneath her bikini.

"What are you doing?" Kandi asked me.

"Just go with it. Trust me," I whispered in her ear.

"I don't know ... ah ..."

My fingers found Kandi's clit and before she could protest any further, I gave Young Reezy an up close view of me playing with Kandi's pussy.

"This is off chain," Reezy yelled as he fondled Kandi's titties. I began to kiss Kandi on her neck as I continued to fondle her. Her pussy got so wet and before she knew it Kandi was having an orgasm right in front of us.

"Oh shit!" Kandi cried out and came. I pulled my fingers out from under her bikini and turned her face and kiss her. She kissed me back as I darted my tongue in and out of her mouth. Pretty soon we forgot that Young Reezy was the one we were supposed to be entertaining. He was enjoying the show. I pulled away and got up off of Reezy and Kandi gave me a look of shock. I smiled then turned my attention to some of the other niggas in the room. After a twenty-minute show we both headed back to the bedroom in the back. I closed and locked the door behind us. Kandi was noticeably quiet.

"You ok girl?" I asked her as I counted the tips I made.

"Yeah. Um … Jasmine," Kandi said nervously and sat on the bed.

"What's up?" I continued to count the tips.

"About what happened out there … ah, I'm not gay. I mean, I like men," Kandi said still in shock.

I stopped counting the money and looked at her. "Okay, so do I. I like you too. You never kissed a girl before," I asked and sat next to her on the bed.

"Yeah I have but nothing like what you did to me."

I grinned. "Did you like it?"

"What?" Kandi asked taken off guard by my question.

"You heard me. Did you like it? I know you did. That kiss wasn't just one way," I said and caressed her thigh. Kandi bit her bottom lip as I moved my hand back up to her crotch. "It felt good didn't it?"

Kandi nodded her head as I rubbed her clit through her bikini. "You want me to make you cum again Kandi?"

Her eyes went from mine, then to my hand, then back to mine. Her breathing became deep then she answered. "Yes … no, I'm not … gay."

"Kandi, haven't you ever been curious about it?" I moved my face toward hers and kissed her. A soft moan escaped her lips and I pushed her willing body back on the bed. I pulled down her bikini and her coochie was nice and creamy. I took off her bikini, spread her thick chocolate legs and licked her swollen clit. Kandi moaned as I continued to lick her slowly. She tasted just as sweet as I thought she would.

The Pink Palace II

Chapter Five

Deal with the Devil

Atlanta, GA
Malachi

She was a beautiful thing, even when she was upset. Since we left the restaurant she hadn't said anything else to me as we rode up Peachtree Road in the limo to the Ritz Carlton. She stared out of the window as I sat across from her drinking my Courvoisier. She kept insisting she loved Dre but still, she was here with me. I knew that deep down inside what she really loved was power.

That's what I represented—power. And as much as she may not want to admit, she was drawn to me. A woman like Nikki wanted a nigga like me in her life.

She just didn't know it yet.

We got to the Ritz and checked into a penthouse suite overlooking Lenox Mall. Still no words were exchanged between us. She walked to the mini bar, took a mini bottle of Smirnoff Vodka and downed it. She looked at me blankly then turned and walked into the bedroom. I took off my jacket, tossed it into a chair and followed behind her.

I walked in and Nikki stood by the oversized bed. She reached up and pulled the strap of her dress over her right shoulder. Then she pulled down the left strap and her dress fell to the floor. Her body was flawless as she stood in front of me in her black lace bra and panties. I walked around her and kissed her on the neck. I unclasped her bra and it fell on top of her dress. I caressed her breasts with both hands and her nipples became hard along with my dick. I laid her on the bed and pulled her panties off. Her long, luscious legs spread exposing her fat pussy.

My tongue snaked up her thigh and tasted her sweet nectar. She tried to fight the feeling but I could tell her body couldn't deny it by how wet she became. I licked her clit from left to right, slurping her juices up. She stifled a moan, and gripped the sheets; still fighting the sensations I gave her.

"You like it don't you?" I asked her but she didn't answer. "I know you do Nikki, I know you do."

I licked her faster. She tried to pull away but I gripped her legs and pulled her back toward me. My tongue swirled around her moist walls. She came in my mouth and her arms flayed on the bed. I continued my tongue stroke as her body jerked involuntarily until she couldn't hold back any more.

"Oh shit … ah, ah, shit," Nikki moaned.

I stood up and unbuckled my belt then pulled down my slacks and boxers. My dick stood long and hard. Nikki was still trying to recover from her orgasm as she lay, spread eagle, on the king size bed. I climbed on top of her and rubbed my shaft with her moistness. I grabbed her face and made her look at me. Then I kissed her. She tried to resist but I wouldn't let her move. Then I pushed my long python inside of her wetness. Damn, she felt so good. She turned her head to the side and closed her eyes as I stroked her hard and deep.

"Look at me," I said as I continued to stroke her. She ignored me. I grabbed her face again. "Look at me!"

She reluctantly obeyed and glared at me. "Dis is my pussy," I asserted and gave her a hard deep stroke and she grunted. "Who's pussy is dis?"

She frowned and bit her bottom lip but didn't answer.

I gave her another hard deep stroke and asked again, "Who's pussy is dis?"

Angrily, she looked at me but spoke it, "Yours."

I smiled and continued to have my way with her for the rest of the night. This pussy belonged to me and soon she would too.

Nikki

I woke up in bed sore from the horrible sex I had with Malachi. I felt so angry with myself for being with him. Even more disgusted for enjoying some of it. I hated myself but I did what I had to for Dre. I heard Malachi in the bathroom showering. I wanted to grab my clothes and leave but I couldn't leave just yet. I needed to shower and wash his funk off of me. Every time that nasty nigga came, he nutted all over me then when he was done, made me sleep in it. I wrapped the bed sheet around my body and got up. Just then, the bathroom door opened and Malachi stood there in his boxers grinning at me.

"Good morning my dear."

I glared at him and didn't answer.

"You were magnificent last night Nikki."

I cut my eyes at him then retorted sarcastically, "I'm glad you enjoyed yourself."

He gave me a shit-eating grin. "Oh I did but I wasn't the only one who did."

"Whatever Malachi. We're done with each other," I affirmed as I walked to the bathroom.

"I thought you said you wanted to make a deal regarding Dre?"

I paused and turned around, "What's there to discuss? We fucked! You got what you wanted from me. What more do you want?"

"That wasn't a deal Nikki. That was sex. What I want from you is much more profitable."

I stood there in shock. What the hell did this nigga want from me?

"What are you talking about?"

"My dear Nikki, I want you to be my number one dancer. I want you at The Pink Palace."

"What? I'm not gonna dance there," I yelled, pissed the fuck off.

Malachi smiled, "You did before."

I was in total shock. "How did you know that?" I asked but he didn't answer. "What does this have to do with Dre?"

"He's in a coma, remember? The doctors don't know his fate, so he may as well be dead. You're just too lovely to let get away. Besides it'll be like a homecoming for you right?" He paused and looked at me smugly. "I did a little research on you darling Nikki and you were the club's number one draw back in the day. You can help Dre settle his debt with me."

I scowled at him. "You're out of your damn mind. I won't do it."

He smiled. "If you want Dre to stay alive you will. You'll be at The Pink Palace Friday night ready to work," Malachi walked up to me and pulled my sheet away. "Yes, you'll definitely be my number one gal. The limo will be waiting for you downstairs when you're done. No worries Nikki, I'm gonna take very good care of you."

I couldn't believe this shit! How did I let this happen to me again? Malachi kissed my lips then turned and picked up his clothes and started to get dressed. I walked into the bathroom, locked the door behind me, turned on the shower and got in. Tears streamed down my face as the hot water washed over me. He would kill Dre if I refused to go back. There was no other option I had. I worked so hard to get away from this life and now I have no choice but to do it again.

I made sure I stayed in the shower extra long before I got out. When I came out of the bathroom Malachi was gone. My dress was laid out on the bed and on top of it were five one hundred dollar bills. He left the cash behind like I was a prostitute. Tears watered my eyes as anger filled my heart. I knocked the bills on the floor and got dressed. I went downstairs and saw a limo out front waiting for me. I don't want to take it but I didn't have any other way of getting home.

🜲 🜲 🜲 🜲 🜲 🜲 🜲 🜲 🜲 🜲 🜲 🜲 🜲 🜲 🜲 🜲

After I got home, I changed clothes and headed to Emory to see Dre. As I drove in the Cutlass my thoughts were all over the place. What did I do? I fucked that grimy ass nigga for what? Now I had to go back and dance my ass off in his club! When I got to Emory, Dre's condition was still the same. Half of me hoped to see him up and waiting for me to come in but the other half knew that wouldn't be true. Instead I walked in, sat by his side and took his hand.

"I'm so sorry Dre," I whispered as I rubbed his hand. "I thought … I thought I could protect you."

Dre looked so peaceful. Please wake up. Just open your eyes for me. I thought of our son and I didn't want him to grow up without a father. I didn't want him to go down the same path so many young black boys traveled without a father figure. What kind of example could I set for him, by me dancing at The Pink Palace?

Just as I was lost in thought about our son's future the door opened and a black female walked in. She was quite beautiful and young.

"Hello, Ms. Bell?" she asked.

"Yes."

"Hi, my name is Dr. Griffin." She shook my hand. I looked at her badge and it read, Dr. Nia Griffin. I hadn't seen too many black females as doctors around the hospital. "I'll be Andre's new doctor."

I was surprised by the sudden change, "Oh, okay. How is he doing?"

She began to look over his chart and checked his vitals, "He's stable and that's the good news. Ms. Bell."

"You can call me Nikki." I looked back at Dre. "How can you all continue to say he's stable and it's good news? The more he lies here, non-responsive, that isn't good news, doctor. Not to me anyway."

The doctor smiled sympathetically and nodded before she answered my question. "Nikki, his body is healing itself. Coma patients are unpredictable. Many wake up on their own. We just don't know when."

"He would wake up or he could die," I reminded her.

"You're right but I'm going to do my best to prevent that." She looked back at him, then at me. "I'm going to give you some more time with him." Dr. Griffin turned and left the room. It was a gut feeling but I did believe she would do everything she could for Dre. Just like I planned to do everything I could to protect him.

Chapter Six

Ego

Atlanta, GA
Jasmine

Another Friday night at The Pink Palace so it was time for me to get that money. I parked and came in through the employee entrance in the back that led to the locker rooms. I got there late but when you were the number one money getter you were always on time. When I walked in, I noticed a few girls getting changed but figured most of them were out front working. I strolled to my dressing table and saw Kandi looking at herself in the mirror adjusting her red babydoll teddy looking like a sexy Bratz doll. I hadn't seen her since the night we hooked up at Young Reezy's party.

She spotted my reflection in the mirror and gave me a shy smile. Once she finished with her outfit, she turned around and walked over to me at my dressing table.

"What's up Jasmine?" Kandi crooned.

I smiled at her and eyed her up and down. "What's up you? You look cute."

"Thanks. I took some of that money I made at the party and bought myself some new outfits."

"Good, cause some that other shit you was wearing before wasn't cutting it," I informed her.

"Oh?" Kandi looked at me oddly. "Jasmine, about what happened at the party ..."

I grinned at her seductively. "We had fun."

"I know ... but I'm not gay," she whispered so the few girls left in the locker room wouldn't be able to hear.

I turned around and looked at her. "Kandi, I know you're not gay. Neither am I. I love me some dick but every now and then I like to taste something sweet." I sat in my chair, checked my fingernails, then stared Kandi in her eyes. "Besides, by the way you were moaning you didn't seem to be too worried about being gay or not."

Kandi blushed, "I know but ..."

"But what?" I retorted and looked at her straightforwardly. "We fucked. No big deal. You're young, sexy and having fun. Besides when was the last time your man made you feel that good?"

"Not in a long time," she answered modestly.

"So there! I ain't trying to turn you out or make you my bitch," I explained with a laugh. She giggled, but if I wanted to, I could. "You're going to have to lighten up girl!"

"Okay … so do you have anymore private parties we can do?"

"I'll let you know." I gave her a wink.

I knew I could have her ass anytime I wanted now. It was always good to have a young tender roni in your pocket. "So what's been going on here?"

"Well … some new chick just started here tonight."

I rolled my eyes. "Another newbie? Great, I hope she stays away from Reggie's horny ass."

"Ah, I don't think she's a newbie," Kandi told me. "Malachi brought her in himself and a lot of the niggas up in here been going crazy for her."

I narrowed my eyes at her. "You said Malachi brought her up in here?"

"Yep. He was giving her the royal treatment and shit. She must be something special," Kandi noted.

I didn't like that shit at all. If any bitch should be getting the royal treatment from Malachi it should've been me! I worked too hard to become the number one money maker to be upstaged by some random bitch Malachi decided to bring in. "Where is this trick?"

Kandi pointed toward the stage. "This is her third encore dance since she's been here. Niggas are wildin' out over her."

"What?!" I fumed and walked toward the stage and looked out. I saw this chick on stage, swinging on the pole like a triathlon! She was good. Ludacris' "My Chick Bad" was blasting and she dropped into a split and made her ass bounce as niggas threw money at her left and right. Sure there were plenty of hoes here who could do the same thing but none them had a body like that. Then I saw her face and it was the same chick who was out to dinner with Malachi the other night.

"Who is this bitch?" I mumbled.

"They call her Nikki," Kandi informed me.

What the hell was Malachi doing? He never took me out to eat or anything! What was so special about her? Who was she really? Obviously by the way she moved she wasn't no newbie. Maybe she was from out of town and Malachi brought her in to make some more money. I had to admit that this Nikki person was a sexy looking bitch with long chocolate legs, a fat, round ass and a flawless face. I watched her for another few minutes until her set was over and I went back to the locker room. I was gonna have to see what was up with her.

Nikki

It was like riding a bike, dancing on this stage again. My mind went on autopilot and my body fell back into the same old freaky gyrations and motions I used to do when I used to dance. Malachi decided to bring me in himself and hype up my return to the Pink Palace. I couldn't stand his ass for blackmailing me back into this shit hole!

As I was walking off stage a strong pair of hands grabbed my arm and pulled me to the side. I knew a nigga didn't have some nerve to put his goddamn hands on me! I may have been gone for a while but not long enough for me not to bust a nigga upside the head!

"What are you doing here?"

I looked at his face and it was Polo, Dre's best friend. Polo's real name was Teddy Williams. He was Dre's best friend since grade school. After Dre got out of the game, Polo took over his spots for him. He was tall and muscular, six foot two brother with butterscotch toned skin. He was lucky I knew him or the Budweiser bottle on the table would have been going over his head.

I yanked my arm away from him. "Polo why you grabbing me like that and what are you doing here?"

"I asked you first."

I rolled my eyes. "What does it look like?"

"Nikki what the hell are you doing here? Dre's in the hospital fighting for his life and you're up in here shaking your ass for the nigga who put him in there," Polo growled.

"You don't understand," I sighed.

"Then explain it to me!"

"Because I'm trying to keep Dre alive is the reason I'm up in here!"

Polo got a confused look on his face. "What?"

"Malachi is making me work off Dre's debt or he'll finish the job," I told him angrily.

Polo shook his head, "Damn it … this is wrong. You can't do this Nikki."

"I have no choice."

"I should've killed that nigga when I had the chance," Polo scowled.

I remembered just a few weeks ago I was telling him to do that but Polo was nowhere as deep as Malachi. He would've been cut down before he could ever get close to him. Just talking to me like he was in the club could've been dangerous for him. I knew Malachi was watching me.

"No, listen Polo I gotta do this," I pleaded with him. "I got this under control so please stay out of it."

"Nikki … you'll never pay back that much money."

"I don't have any choice," I told him.

"Nikki—"

"I have to go." I walked back to the lockers.

I had to get away from him before Malachi started asking who he was to me and found out his connection to Dre. I didn't need another person I knew to get hurt by Malachi. As I walked into the locker room a lot of the girls gave me the stink eye. A few I recognized but most I didn't. They didn't like the fact that I was back. Neither did I but I had to do what I had to do. This one chick stood across the room and smirked at me oddly. She was a pretty redbone with high cheekbones, big titties and a small waist. I could tell right away she was the head bitch at the palace. The same way I was when I was here before.

I pretended to not notice her staring at me and walked over to my locker. I started to count my money as she and some other little brown skinned chick walked toward me. I tucked my money away in my bag and closed my locker.

"Hey, you looked real good out there," the redbone chick said to me slyly.

"Thanks," I replied cautiously.

"Listen, they call me Jasmine. This here is Kandi."

I looked over to Kandi and she gave me a blank stare.

"I'm Nikki."

"Well Nikki, I see you've made quite the first impression out there but you should know I'm the Queen Bitch here at the Pink Palace. So any thoughts you might be having about coming up in here and taking over you can forget it."

I rolled my eyes. "Well Queen Bee, you can relax. I'm only here to get this paper. You can have the groupies.

Most of the guys here know me and know how I get down."

She squinted her eyes. "Know you? You've been here before?"

I gathered my belongings off of my dressing table. "Yeah you can say that. Like I said, I'm only here for this paper."

Just as I began to walk away to head toward the exit, Jasmine blurted something that I didn't expect.

"And Malachi?"

I turned and stared at her. She must've been sucking his dick and thought I was gonna take away her meal ticket. Fuck Malachi. She could have him. Instead of acknowledging her, I turned back around and walked out of the lockers without another word.

Chapter Seven

Special Circumstances

Atlanta, GA
Malachi

Watching Nikki on stage was almost as arousing as fucking her. Even though she wouldn't give herself to me completely she was still exceptional. My dumb ass brother was supposed to kill Dre but instead he put him in a coma which brought Nikki's fine ass straight to me. I promised to let that nigga live if she worked for me but if that nigga woke up I'd kill him anyway. Which was a win-win situation for me.

My cellular chimed and I answered the line, "Talk."

"We have a problem Malachi," Ricky informed.

"I pay you to solve problems."

He swallowed hard, "I will, but you should know—"

"Not over the phone. Where are you?"

"At the spot."

"Come here now," I directed him.

"On my way." Ricky ended the call.

It must've been a situation if Ricky felt the need to call me. Another problem that I'd have to address as if the fucking police weren't stressing me out enough. Good thing I had Detective Raymond on my payroll keeping the heat off me. Now if somebody could keep my damn baby mama Latoya out of my ass, things would be perfect. I swear if it weren't for my daughter I would have made her dig a hole for herself. I decided to smoke my ganja to relax my nerves when Bump rang my line.

"What is it?"

"Jasmine wants to see you boss," Bump replied.

"Send her in."

Bump opened the door and Jasmine sashayed her sexy ass inside. Her ass was hanging out of her red boy shorts. Her big ass titties looked nice and ripe like mangos with her hard nipples protruding out of her bikini top. Jasmine was one sexy bitch. She sat her fat ass on my desk and pursed her lips together. Her eyes looked out my window.

I leaned back in my chair. "What can I do for you my dear?"

"You can tell me who that bitch is," Jasmine inquired pointing toward my window. The jealously was obvious. Most girls in here couldn't hold a candle to Jasmine but Nikki was just as sexy.

"That's Nikki," I replied.

"That much I know already," she frowned. "Why did you bring her up in here? I thought I was your number one girl?"

"Nikki is here under special circumstances. Nothing you need to concern yourself with," I explained to her.

Jasmine folded her arms and glared at me. "So those special circumstances include dinner with you?"

I glared back at her. "Yes. Yuh have a problem wit dat?"

Hearing the change in my voice, she gave me a nervous smile realizing that questioning what I do was not wise.

"No … it's just … I was just curious as to why she's getting special treatment," she mumbled.

I stood up and caressed my fingers down the side of one of Jasmine's full breasts. I tugged on her bikini top making her titty pop out. My thumb rubbed over her hard nipple as my anaconda grew harder. She smiled, and undid her top revealing her succulent breasts. She stood up and I pulled her boy shorts down over her fat ass.

"Whatcha want daddy?" she purred.

"You," I told her and undid my pants. I pulled out my black anaconda, stroked the beast and sat back down in my chair. Jasmine turned around and sat her ass down in my lap gently easing my massive dick into her wet pussy. Damn … she felts so fucking warm. She slid up and down my shaft like a stripper pole. She put her hands on my desk and wound her waistline around and around pushing her ass back.

"Oh … shit daddy. You feel so good," she crooned.

"Ride it … yes … just like dat you sexy bitch," I moaned and slapped her ass.

"Ow… ah … ah …" Jasmine groaned as I grabbed her hips and worked my pipe up the middle of her pum-pum. Hard and fast I stroked as I pushed her forward and stood behind her so I could get up in it further. I glanced back behind me through the club window and spotted Nikki dancing and imagined it was her I was fucking again.

"Damn Malachi … you fucking the shit outta me," Jasmine cried as I banged her back in. The sound of my dick smacking her pussy filled my office. Her face was down on top of my desk as I had her bent over. Feeling my nut coming, I withdrew from her pussy and spewed my seed on her backside. I groaned deeply as I emptied my shaft. I wouldn't make the same bloodclot mistake again cumming inside of one of these bitches and having another baby. That's how I got stuck with Latoya's ass in the first place.

"Go clean yourself up," I told Jasmine as I tucked my dick back in my boxers and zipped up.

"Okay baby … and uh." She held out her hand just like a greedy bitch. Money was never too far off of her mind. I reached in my pocket and took two G's off of my money clip and tossed it on the desk. She scooped it up while she was still bent over my desk. She stood up and counted the money as my cum ran down the crack of her ass. She took some napkins off my desk and wiped her ass off then started to dress herself. I sat back down in my chair still enjoying the aftershocks of my orgasm.

"So you're going to be at the grand opening of my new club next month?"

She grinned, "Of course. As long as I'm the headliner making top dollar."

"Of course," I confirmed.

"Good, cause you know I'm the best," she boasted. "And not some other chick."

I picked up my blunt and relit it. All these bitches think their pussy is better than the next bitch. Too bad for Jasmine, Nikki's pussy was on my mind while I fucked her.

"You can leave now."

Jasmine tucked her money in her bikini top and left my office. I turned in my chair and looked at Nikki again. I was going to have her ass again … real soon.

♛ ♛ ♛ ♛ ♛ ♛ ♛ ♛ ♛ ♛ ♛ ♛ ♛ ♛ ♛ ♛

Thirty minutes later Ricky came up in the club and made his way to my office. He told me there was a problem over the phone so he better explain. Nobody better be fucking up my money. He walked in and had a seat in front of my desk.

"What's bloodclot problem?"

Ricky sighed. "Jorge is dead."

"A pure fuckery dat!"

Ricky shook his head, "Yeah Malachi. Somebody wiped out Jorge and his whole crew and took our shit. They were five men deep and when we got there they all were Swiss cheesed up."

"Twenty kilos of coke gone? bloodclot!" I snapped. "What'cha telling me Ricky? What pussyclot stupid enough to romp wit me?"

"I don't know but I'm already on it. I got muthafuckas on the streets checking shit out. One of these small time niggas might be trying to grow some balls."

"Well," I glared at Ricky in the eyes. "You better cut them fucking off."

Jasmine

Well, that didn't accomplish shit! Malachi ain't saying shit about whatever him and this Nikki got going on. Instead, all he gave me was some stiff dick and a sore pussy. At least I got some cash for my services but I was even more curious about what special circumstances Nikki got going on. As I was walking down the stairs from Malachi's office I spotted Reggie harassing some girls again. Then I thought about it. Malachi might not wanna tell me what's going on with Nikki but I bet I can get dumb ass Reggie to give me some info. I walked over to him.

"What's up Reggie?"

He turned and glared at me, "I ain't bothering nobody Jasmine."

I smiled, "Did I say you were? I was just saying what's up."

"Oh, okay," he replied, confused by my kindness.

"I see there's a new dancer here now. Calls herself Nikki. You know her?"

"Yeah … Nikki used to dance here a few years ago. Looks like she got thicker too. Her and this other chick," Reggie squinted as if searching his memory bank, "this other chick named Mo'Nique used to trick up in here before they quit."

"You knew her back then?"

"Not really … I just used to come up in here and watch them hoes dance. Nikki used to fuck with all the big time hustlers that used to come up in here. Why? You feeling a little intimidated by her?" Reggie asked sarcastically.

I rolled my eyes, "Hell naw, I just wanted to know

who she is."

Reggie picked up his beer off the table and took a sip. "So Jasmine you gonna give me a dance at my birthday party next month?"

I eyed him up and down. "You know my fee. As long as the money is right I might."

"Shit! I got that. How much more I gotta give you for a private dance that night?"

I cut my eyes at him, "What you trying to ask me Reggie?"

"I know you fucking my brother so I just wanna know how can I be down?"

"You can't afford me nigga." Instead of cussing his ass out, I turned and walked away from his ugly behind. He gave me more info I didn't know about this Nikki chick, so I couldn't be that mad at him. So, she used to dance here years ago and now she's back. Why?

Chapter Eight

Disappearing Act

College Park, GA
Nikki

My body was so damn sore. I hadn't danced like that since I worked here last and I wasn't as young as I used to be. I didn't get in until four in the morning and I had been dancing at The Pink Palace all week. It was a good thing I had Penny working for me at the store cause I didn't think I could've made it in if I were tired. Seeing Polo at the club the other night did not help things at all. The look on his face when he saw me was of total disgust. He was Dre's best friend but didn't realize I was doing this for him. Fucking Malachi was making me his dance slave to spare Dre's life.

My iPhone started to play Alicia Keys, "Try Sleeping With A Broken Heart" and I rolled over and look at the display and saw Janelle's name. Shit. It was 8:10 AM and she had Tyler for me last night. Between her and Penny they've been helping me take care of him since Dre got hurt. I was supposed to pick him up so Janelle could get to work on time.

I pushed the accept button on my phone, "Janelle, I'm on my way cuz ... I over slept!"

"It's okay Nikki ... I'm off today," Janelle calmly replied.

"Oh ... I feel like crap."

"How come? You're still not sleeping because of Dre?"

If only she knew. "Yeah, it's because of Dre."

"Tell you what Nikki, let's meet today for lunch at Taco Mac in midtown," Janelle suggested.

"Okay, about 12:30?"

"Sounds good. I'll bring Tyler."

"Thanks Janelle. I don't know how I'd get through all this without you."

"Nikki, you were there for me when I needed you. I'll always be there for you. I'll see you later."

"Alright cuz."

When she hung up, I put my hands over my face. What have I gotten myself into?

♛ ♛ ♛ ♛ ♛ ♛ ♛ ♛ ♛ ♛ ♛ ♛ ♛ ♛ ♛

Two hours later I rolled my ass out of bed and staggered to the shower. The warm water felt good over my sore muscles. I never used to feel like this back in the day. Of course I was doing it every other night and that was pre-baby, but I didn't lose anything when it came to dancing. I still shook my ass with the best of them. The only problem was that Jasmine chick thought I was there to take her spot. Shit ... she could have it. If this was the old me I woulda been shut her ass down but the only thing that kept me there was Malachi holding Dre's life over my head.

I had been so caught up dancing at the Palace again that I hadn't had time to go check on Dre. Look at me lying to myself. I hadn't gone to see Dre because I felt ashamed of doing this shit again. A life I swore to him I was done with. Didn't matter though. After I met Janelle for lunch I was gonna take Tyler to go visit his daddy. I didn't want him to forget who he was.

♛ ♛ ♛ ♛ ♛ ♛ ♛ ♛ ♛ ♛ ♛ ♛ ♛ ♛ ♛ ♛ ♛

An hour later I drove in to midtown Atlanta to Taco Mac on Peachtree Street and found a spot in the parking garage. When I walked into the restaurant I saw Janelle with Tyler sitting at a booth waiting for me. Janelle had ordered some fries and was feeding them to Tyler. He looked so much like his father. Janelle had him in a high chair dressed in his little blue overalls and a mini red polo shirt. He was munching away at his fries when he looked up and spotted me.

"Mommy!" He beamed.

"Hey baby," I crooned and kissed him. "You been a good boy for Auntie Janelle?"

He smiled, "Yes."

"He's been a very good boy Nikki," Janelle confirmed. "He loves his auntie!"

I had a seat at the table.

"I can't thank you enough for taking him for the night."

Janelle looked at me oddly. "You know Jayson and I don't mind watching our godson but this was the third time this week Nikki. Is everything okay?"

I smiled nervously, "I'm fine. It's just with Dre gone I've had to work some extra hours at the store."

"Really Nikki ... cause last time I was there Penny told me you were taking some time off and she was running the store. You've been kind of MIA this whole week. So what's really going on?"

Janelle was no dummy. She knew me better than I knew myself sometimes. The waitress walked up to the table giving me an escape from her question. After we placed our orders I turned my attention to Tyler.

"Nikki ..."

"I'm going to take Tyler to see Dre this afternoon," I told her before she asked the question again.

"That's good but you're avoiding my question. What's going on with you?"

I sighed, "Janelle ... I ..." I looked at her watching me for an answer. I didn't want to lie to her but I couldn't tell her the truth right now. "I can't tell you."

She pursed her lips together, "Me? You can't tell me of all people? Nikki what the hell is going on?" She looked at me concerned. "If you're in trouble I wanna help."

"I'm not in trouble. I just need to handle this by myself. Listen, Janelle, you have your own life now and you have Jayson. I was foolish enough to get you involved in life years ago and it was the wrong thing to do. Trust me, when the time is right I'll let you know what's up but for right now just let me handle this," I begged.

Janelle looked at me and sighed. I knew she wanted to help me regardless, but Malachi was just way too dangerous for her to get mixed up with.

"Okay," she shook her head. "I'ma let you do what you need to do for now but you're going to tell me everything soon. You're my family and I love you Nikki. Anything that affects you affects me."

"I know."

"Besides, you have to worry about Tyler now. He needs you more than ever."

"I'll do whatever I need to do in order to protect him Janelle. You don't have to worry about that," I assured her. And I'll do anything to protect Dre too, I thought to myself.

👑 👑 👑 👑 👑 👑 👑 👑 👑 👑 👑 👑 👑 👑 👑

After we finished up lunch Janelle went home and I drove to Emory Hospital a few blocks away from Taco Mac with Tyler. I hated not telling Janelle what was going on with me but it was for her own good. I took the elevator to Dre's floor and carried Tyler in my arms to his room. When I walked, my heart dropped into my stomach. I nearly dropped Tyler as well. My eyes scanned the room from left to right but it was empty. Dre was gone!

Chapter Nine

Marked For Death

Buckhead, GA
Malachi

I decided to take my daughter Courtney to Lenox Mall to buy her a few things and of course Latoya had to bring her ass along too. The only two things her ass were good for was lying on her back and spending my money. At least this little shopping spree would shut her bumbaclot mouth and keep her out of my hair. I had other concerns on my mind, like what pussyhole had the nerve to rob a shipment of cocaine from me.

Whoever they were killed Jorge and his men and took my shit! Even more disturbing was that they knew where Ricky was going to meet Jorge, which told me this was an inside job. I didn't trust no man so anybody could be a suspect. Lucky for Ricky I knew he wasn't involved because the eyes I had watching him were in his crew. So that meant somebody else was doing this. My brother Reggie wasn't smart enough to pull this off without fucking it up so that took him off my list. So who else was that fucking stupid?

As I was lost in thought thinking about this situation, Latoya walked up to me in Neiman Marcus with her hand out, "Give me your card."

I glared at her, "What did you say to me?"

She rolled her eyes, "I gotta pay for these clothes."

"You mean I gotta pay for these clothes. Watch how you ask me for my card."

"Whatever," she said and rolled her neck. "Shit gotta be paid for."

"Watch you bloodclot mouth," I growled through clinched teeth. I wanted to snap her neck right there in the store.

"Or what? You gonna hit me? The mother of yo child," she dared.

She didn't know how close to the edge she was. "Yuh stupid bitch—"

Her eyes bugged out of her head. "Oh no you didn't just talk to me like that!"

"Keep pushing me Toya, and you have no idea how close you are …"

"You another one of them crazy ass Jamaican men Malachi," she quipped. "You don't want the drama I'ma bring to you if you put your hands on me."

I grabbed her by her arm and snatched her closer to me. Latoya was shocked and fear replaced the arrogance in her face. My grip was so strong I could have yanked her arm out of its socket.

"Ow ... you're hurting me Malachi!" Pain was etched in her face.

"I know and I don't give a damn. Don't think for a second you're untouchable because you can come up missing one day," I uttered to her menacingly. Her eyes widened like saucers as my message became clear to her.

"Mommy I wanna go," Courtney yelled saving her mother.

I let her go and she pulled herself together before Courtney realized the tension between us. "Okay baby, I was just asking your daddy for something."

I handed her my black card and Courtney ran up to me and hugged my leg.

"Daddy can you buy me some ice cream too!"

"Anything for my baby," I said to her and smiled. "Go with your mother to the register." I glared at Latoya. "I'm going to go to the restroom downstairs."

"Okay Daddy," Courtney beamed.

"I'll meet you in the food court," I told Latoya and she nodded nervously.

I walked out of the store cause I had to get away from that bitch before I killed her. She thought just because she was my child's mother she could romp wit me. Nobody romps with Malachi Turner!

I went to the lower level of the mall, walked through the food court, and went to the men's restroom. As I walked in I noticed a nigga behind me dressed in khakis and a plaid, blue, button down come in behind me. His fro was nappy, skin was reddish toned, and he was well built. He stuck out in my mind. I walked all the way to the end of restroom to the last urinal and he went into a stall. I heard him pissing so I did the same. I was on edge and felt paranoid. Latoya had me unfocused. I swear that bitch would be the death if me if I didn't kill her first. I went to wash my hands and splashed some water on my face. Had to remain calm.

Then I saw the red nigga again behind me in the mirror walking up on me quick. His hands went underneath his shirt, pulled out a blade and with one swift motion stabbed forward. I barely had time to move and get my guard up. The knife stabbed my left bicep. Blood sprayed the restroom mirror. He was aiming for my neck. Pain shot through my body but I didn't scream out loud. Before he could pull the knife out of me I tagged him with a nasty right to the jaw sending him to the floor. I staggered back. He recovered quickly and was on his feet. We mean mugged each other for a second then I yanked the blade out of my arm and threw it on the ground behind me.

"Who sent yuh?"

He didn't respond but instead he pulled out a second blade and attacked me again. He slashed at my face but I avoided his attack. I could feel my blood soaking my arm. He slashed at me again and I grabbed his arm. My other hand grabbed his neck as he gasped for air. I was trying to crush his windpipe. Physically, I was bigger, stronger and meaner. I slammed him into the mirror, head first, shattering it. He dropped the second blade into the sink underneath him. Then I repeatedly smashed his head against the broken glass. He tried to break my grip but it was too strong. Someone sent a man to kill a beast.

"Who fuckin' sent yuh?" I yelled smashing his head again against the mirror. A bloody smear painted the glass behind him.

He grimaced, "Fuck you!"

My hand squeezed tighter cutting off his air supply and his face began to turn blue. I decided to return the favor and picked up the blade out of the sink and stabbed him in the arm. He let out an excruciating groan. Then I took the blade and entered his stomach repeatedly. I dropped him on top of the counter top. He fought for his last breath before I slashed his throat open, letting the red crimson in his neck fill the white sink.

I had to move fast. I didn't know if there were more assassins waiting for me. I picked up both of his blades and put them in my pocket. My fingerprints were on them and I couldn't leave them behind. I ripped my sleeve off and wrapped it around my bicep in an attempt to stop the bleeding. Then it hit me. Courtney. She was here in the mall with killers after me. I pulled out my gun from the small of my back underneath my shirt. I didn't need it to deal with dis pussyhole but I didn't know who else was out there for me. I grabbed my cell, dialed Bump's number, and he answered on the first ring. He was in the car in the parking lot.

"Boss—"

"Get in here! Niggas are here to kill me," I growled to him.

"Where are you?"

"The food court! I'm coming out now! Protect my daughter," I commanded as I crept out of the restroom door. I hung up.

I was covered in blood and holding a gun. I was going to have to move fast. A woman walked by and stared at me oddly. When I mean-mugged her, she quickly moved on. I walked quickly through the food court to the exit tucking my gun under my shirt. I spotted Latoya and Courtney sitting at a table waiting for me. She was safe but then I saw danger.

The red nigga wasn't alone. I spotted four of them by the exits looking at me. They were wearing shades and dressed in big jackets. Bumba clot … my daughter was in the middle. I moved to the other side of the food court through the crowd of people. The killers moved with me away from Latoya and Courtney. Another person noticed my bloody arm and pointed me out to his friend. I brushed by a few more people and the assassins closed in on me. They were twenty-five maybe thirty feet away and weren't going to let me escape so I decided to draw first blood. I aimed my cannon and let thunder explode from the barrel. I hit a killer in the face giving him a closed casket funeral. Blood sprayed all over people walking by.

"Bring it on pussyholes!" I yelled.

Pandemonium erupted as the people in the food court shrieked and ran for cover. The killers pulled out their steel and returned my hollow tips. Men screamed like bitches. Bodies hit the ground as I dove behind the counter of an Auntie Anne's Pretzels. Mayhem had just begun to let loose as Lenox Mall turned into Afghanistan. Bullets couldn't tell who was an innocent bystander in this war. Pools of blood covered the floor as the gunmen took cover behind pillars and restaurant counters. Balls of fire flew over my head. They had me boxed in. I only had a few more bullets in my clip. Death was closing in on me.

"Yuh coming for me," I defiantly shouted. "Yuh bumba clot coming for me? Yuh want to murda me? Come get me pussyholes! I got hot fire for yuh asshole!

I murda yuh all!"

I should have seen this coming. My heart dropped into my belly as I saw her.

"Daddy," Courtney yelled, as she broke free from Latoya and ran into the middle of the food court.

A gunman turned and aimed his cannon at her. He looked at me then smiled.

Nikki

Dre was gone. His room looked like it hadn't been occupied in days. Fear washed over me and I quickly ran out of the room with Tyler in my arms. I spotted a nurse walking by.

"Where's Andre?" I yelled frantically.

"Ma'am?"

"Andre Wade! He was in room 415!"

She tried to hold me. "Ma'am calm down."

I pulled away from her. "Don't tell me to calm down; tell me where my man is!"

I didn't care how loud or how rude I was. I wanted answers. Tears filled my eyes and Tyler started to cry to see me so distressed.

"Okay, let me find out," the nurse said calmly and rushed off toward the nurses' station. He couldn't have died. Wouldn't I have been called? I hugged Tyler tightly and he put his arms around me as tears ran down my face. I didn't know if he was trying to console me or if I was trying to calm him down.

"Miss, miss," the nurse called to me. "Miss Bell?"

"Yes, where's my fiancé?"

"Two days ago, Andre Wade was taken into protective

custody by the FBI."

"The FBI?" I repeated. "Why?"

"The FBI said because they found the same shell casing at the scene of a homicide that were used in his shooting they decided to keep him somewhere undisclosed."

I looked at the nurse and yelled, "I don't give a damn about some shells found at a crime scene. Andre is my child's father! How will I know if he is alright?!"

She looked at me and shook her head. I could tell she wanted to give me more information, but didn't have any to give. "Ma'am you'll have to contact the FBI."

She turned and walked away and I was left even more confused than ever. On one hand, I should've been glad Dre was under protection but I had no idea where he was. I had to find out where he was but in the meantime I wasn't going to concern myself with pleasing Malachi. He could kiss my ass!

Chapter Ten

Relaxers

Buckhead, GA
Malachi

A gunman turned and aimed his cannon at Courtney and thunder erupted. The sound of an AK47 ripping through flesh and leaving brain matter all over the food court floor came next. Bump followed my orders to the letter and protected Courtney by murdering the gunman aiming for her. The other two assassins decided to break out and escaped through a restaurant exit.

"Daddy!" Courtney looked around confused and scared.

"Courtney!" Latoya yelled and ran to her.

I jumped over the counter and ran to her as well. She

hugged me tight.

"Boss! We have to go," Bump advised. I looked around and saw bodies all around us. Some dead, others wounded.

"Yes, you did good," I told him. I looked at Latoya and she was shook. "Come!"

We ran out of the mall with Bump leading the way to the parking lot and jumped in the back of the Bentley. Bump burned out of the mall parking lot and within minutes we were on the Georgia 400 north heading to a safe house. Latoya was still holding Courtney tight; neither one saying a word. My little girl had seen death for the first time. Her innocence was lost. As silence enveloped the car we all heard a knocking noise coming from the trunk.

"What is that?" Latoya asked me.

"Bump, what's in the back?"

"After you called me I spotted a nigga in the parking lot with a gat waiting. So I crept up on him and knocked his ass out and put him in the trunk. Figured you may wanna ask him some questions."

"Yes, I have a few questions indeed."

♛ ♛ ♛ ♛ ♛ ♛ ♛ ♛ ♛ ♛ ♛ ♛ ♛ ♛ ♛ ♛ ♛

Twenty minutes later we arrived at a safe house in Alpharetta. Couldn't take a chance of going home to Dunwoody cause there would have been more killers waiting for me. I called Ricky and Reggie and told them where to meet me and to bring the crew. This was now a war and I needed my soldiers. I called my personal doctor to clean and stitch up my wound. He arrived within a half an hour.

After the doctor took care of me, I made sure Courtney and Latoya were safely settled in the house then I went down to the basement where Bump was working on the asshole that came to murder me. I went downstairs with a plastic bag filled with things I needed and the fool was tied to a chair as Bump pounded his face with his massive fists. The bastard was tough. He was still mean-mugging Bump and not saying a word. I wanted answers. I needed to know who came after me and simply killing this nigga wasn't what I needed to happen.

"Bump." He paused and looked at me. "What has he said?"

"Nothing … yet."

Just then Ricky and Reggie came down the stairs and joined us.

"Boss, who's this?" Ricky asked, looking at the man then back at me.

"One of the pussyholes who came to murda me."

"All the news channels are talking about what went down at Lenox Mall, Malachi. They calling it a blood bath," Reggie informed me.

"Any mention of me?"

"No. They don't have any video or anything posted yet. The police are still investigating it," Ricky answered.

I turned and looked at the nigga in the chair. "Who hired you?"

He didn't say anything and Bump punched him again but he barely grunted. Nothing was fazing this nigga.

"Don't waste your energy Bump. A nigga like him won't break like dis." I walked up on him and stared at his bruised and battered face. His bald head had lumps too. "But yuh will tell me what I need to know and this is your last chance."

"Fuck you! You may as well go ahead and kill me now," he snarled.

I grinned at him. "Yuh waan tess me?"

From the bag I brought downstairs with me, I retrieved a pair of plastic gloves and put one on my right hand. Then I reached back into the plastic bag and took out a bottle of Courtney's Dark and Lovely kid perms and the nigga in the chair looked at me oddly.

"Malachi ... what the fuck you gonna do with that?" Reggie inquired.

I didn't answer him. I took my hand with the glove on it and scooped out a hand full of the white cream and slapped it on the nigga's bald head.

"What the fuck you doing?" he yelled.

Bump grabbed him and held him still as I smeared the cream all over his head. Soon his head top was covered with the creamy white relaxer.

"I'll be back in an hour and we'll see if yuh still waan romp wit me."

"Fuck you man!"

I smiled and peeled off the glove and tossed it on the floor. Bump, Reggie and Ricky followed me back up the stairs.

"I don't get it, what did you do that for?" Reggie asked.

"You'll see."

An hour later I heard an excruciating scream coming from the basement. I marched back down the stairs with

Big Bump, Reggie, and Ricky and saw that nigga on his side, still tied to the chair, trying to rub the relaxer cream off of his head with no success. The chemical burns on his head were literally peeling away the flesh on his scalp as red blisters covered his head. He was yelling and crying like a baby for relief.

"Get it off! GET IT OFF," he shouted.

"Yuh feel like talking yet? Or do yuh waan tess me?"

"Yes! Please! Aarrgh," he squealed.

"Give me a name."

"Don P! Don P!"

I looked at Ricky and Reggie to see if they have heard of a Don P and both of them shook their head no. "Never heard of him."

"Please! He's called Don P! Please get it off me," he begged.

He wasn't lying but the name Don P meant nothing to me. "Where is he from?"

"What?!" I could see the pain in his eyes.

"Is he local?" I asked him.

"I don't know! He … argh … just calls us and wires money to our accounts!"

I looked at him in agony on the floor and realized he had no information worthwhile for me. He was just a hired gun sent to murda me. I still had no idea who was coming for me. This was a fucking waste of time.

"Alright, I believe you." I looked at Bump, "Take care of him."

Bump pulled out his 45.

The nigga's eyes widened. "What? But I told you—"

Thunder exploded from the end of the barrel. Bump

put three slugs in his chest and ended his misery. I still had no answers but I did have a name.

I turned and faced Ricky, "Find out who the fuck Don P is and mash 'em up."

Ricky nodded, "I'm on it Boss."

Jasmine

"Breaking news, three hours ago, gang violence erupted in Lenox Mall killing six people. Included in the dead are three gunmen. We were also told one victim was found in the restroom stabbed to death. Police have made no arrests in the incident. Witnesses are saying a black man opened fire in the middle of the Lenox food court killing a man. Three other men dressed in black drew weapons and returned fire. We will bring you more updates on this breaking story as more information comes in," the news reporter on Channel 2 announced as I put on my jacket.

What the fuck is wrong with these young niggas these days? You can't even go to the fucking mall without catching a bullet in your ass. I turned off the TV and grabbed my keys. I was on my way to make some money at The Pink Palace and was running late. My mind was still wondering what the connection between Malachi and Nikki was and if it was going to interfere with my hustle at the club.

I got to The Pink Palace thirty minutes later and the fucking place was half empty! Where the hell was everybody? It was Saturday night and the place should've been jumping by now. I glanced on stage and saw a couple of chicks on stage poppin' their pussy for a few niggas but that looked like chump change to me. I looked up toward Malachi's office and nobody was there. I headed backstage to see who all was here. As I walked in the dressing room I saw Kandi with three other bitches around sitting at her dressing table laughing and carrying on like it was happy hour or some shit.

Hmp, I guess Kandi finally came out of her shell and made some so-called friends. She was sitting in this one chick's lap named Hester. Hester was a Filipino bitch who looked like a thicker version of the singer Cassie without the half shaven head. The other two bitches were Jade, a curvy chocolate honey with a weave all the way down to her ass and Safire, a thick ass redbone with titties so big that they could give shade to a small child. Kandi had no idea how scandalous these hoes were.

I cleared my throat and Kandi turned and spotted me, "Hey Jasmine." She got up off of Hester's lap. Hester rolled her eyes at me but wisely didn't say shit to me. They knew I didn't play that shit. I was the queen bitch here and everybody recognized. Jade and Safire smirked and giggled to themselves.

"Hey, what's going on?"

"Nothing, we're just here chillin'," Kandi responded nervously.

Hester rose up out of her seat. "We'll holla at you later Kandi."

"Okay."

Hester, Jade, and Safire walked away from us still giggling and shit.

"What the hell is so funny?" I asked Kandi.

She shrugged her shoulders, "I don't know."

I know it shouldn't have bothered me but Kandi was kind of my protégé and I didn't like the way those hoes were all up on her. I didn't like the idea of anybody taking advantage of her, other than me. Just looking at Kandi, she seemed a bit off to me for some reason.

"You better be careful around them hoes."

"Them," she pointed in their direction, "they're harmless."

I walked over to my mirror and took off my jacket, "You think so?"

"We were just hanging out. What's so bad about them?"

"Nothing is wrong with them until they got your ass buck naked in a Booty Talk DVD eating them out."

"Like you did me," she retorted.

I turned and look at her. Since when did she come slick to me? Kandi caught my vibe and looked away.

"I mean ... we were just kicking it. Ain't anybody out there in the club anyway."

"Hmp, true." She was definitely a little off and I could see why by the white dust on her dressing table. "By the way you got a little powder on your nose."

Kandi got a stunned look on her face and wiped her nose.

"If you gonna do that shit then I suggest you be a little more discreet about it. Them hoe's will get your ass open and hooked on that shit if you ain't careful."

"Oh ... okay," she sheepishly replied.

"When was the last time you talked to your boyfriend?" I asked her as I sat in the chair and checked myself in the mirror.

Kandi flopped down in the chair next to me, "A few days ago ... maybe a week. I thought you said I should forget that nigga."

"Yeah, but maybe I spoke too soon." I turned to look

at her. "Listen Kandi, I ain't your mother but just be careful fucking with these bitches around here."

"Okay," Kandi said half-heartedly.

Anyway, I didn't want to waste more time babysitting this girl because it was time to make some money. I got undressed and put on my pink teddy and a pair of red Steve Madden stilettos and reapplied my makeup. Once I was pleased with what I saw in the mirror I made my way back out front of the club but it was still half dead. I walked over to the bar and Gina, the bartender, made me my usual Long Island Iced Tea. Gina was the only chick in the club I trusted. She had a body like a stripper but not the mentality of one.

"What the fuck is going on Gina? Where is everybody?"

"I'm not sure Jasmine but I keep on hearing rumors about somebody in the streets beefing with Malachi."

"Really?" I took sip of my drink. "Who would really want it with him?"

"Don't know, but I hear there was a big hit on some Mexican drug dealers the other night and they were supplying Malachi," she informed me.

I took another sip of my drink. "Hmmm, that's not good. Folks are probably scared to come up in here."

"Plus there was some shit that went down at Lenox Mall this afternoon that's got everybody buzzing."

"I heard about that on the news before I left," I told her.

Just then the club doors opened and Bump was leading the way with Malachi behind him followed by Reggie, Ricky, and ten or twelve other niggas marching up toward his office. Malachi had a scowl on his face like I never saw before. Bump scanned the club and posted niggas strategically. Malachi headed up to his office and Bump, Ricky, and Reggie go with him. Damn. I never saw Malachi with so much security around him before but then it dawned on me that the shoot out that went down in Lenox … could Malachi have been there?

Chapter Eleven

Obsessed With Me

College Park, GA
Nikki

I had been calling the police and FBI for hours and nobody would give me any information about Dre. This was crazy! How could they move him and not tell his family where? I could at least assume he was safe but it still killed me inside that I didn't know where he was. I sat back in my chair in the living room as Tyler watched Marvel Superhero Squad on Cartoon Network.

The more I thought about the situation the more I realized I had no reason to ever return to the Pink Palace. I was supposed to be there tonight but fuck that and fuck Malachi! He couldn't hold Dre's life over my head anymore. The FBI was probably hot on his tail! Good. It felt like it had been a long time since I spent the night home with Tyler. It was past his bedtime but he was enjoying his show so much I didn't want to pull him away. Besides I enjoyed watching him be a kid.

The past few weeks being back at The Pink Palace brought back so many bad memories. I couldn't believe how deluded I was into thinking that being a stripper/ hoe at the club was my calling in life. The stupid shit I did for money and all the low life pigs I fucked with to get it. I even dragged my poor cousin Janelle into that fucked up lifestyle. Talk about the blind leading the blind. I was so glad Dre never gave up on me. He loved me with my flaws and all and we helped each other turn our lives around. We had a son. We had a new life. And now because of Malachi he wasn't here.

A few minutes later Tyler's show went off and I picked him up. "It's time for bed big guy."

"Ok. Where's Daddy?" Tyler asked.

I stared at him and I honestly didn't know what to say to him. "He's … working baby. He'll be home soon." I wished that were the truth. "Come on baby, do you wanna sleep in Mommy's bed tonight?"

He nodded his head and I took him up to my room.

♛ ♛ ♛ ♛ ♛ ♛ ♛ ♛ ♛ ♛ ♛ ♛ ♛ ♛ ♛ ♛

I spent the weekend at home with Tyler catching up on being a mother. My thoughts were still with Dre but I had no idea where to turn. Neither the police nor the FBI were turning my calls. I had to figure out what was going on but I had no idea how.

The next day I dropped Tyler off at the babysitter's

and headed to the shop. When I walked in, Penny saw me and her jaw nearly hit the floor. It had been a while since I had been in and she had been running things pretty good. She was behind the counter ringing a customer out.

"Nikki, I must be dreaming! I wasn't expecting to see you here today!"

"I know, right?" I walked behind the counter and gave her a hug. "I didn't think I would be here today either."

After her customer walked out of the store Penny looked at me. "So what's going on with you and Malachi?"

I frowned and sat on the stool next to Penny. "Forget that nigga, I got bigger concerns."

"Like what? Has something happened to Dre?"

I shook my head and didn't know where to begin. "Dre has been put in protective custody and the FBI won't tell me where he is."

"What?! How can they do that and not tell you?"

"That's what I'm trying to figure out. I've been calling them since Friday but they won't give me any information. I'm so worried about him Penny. I have no idea what condition he was in. If he's awake or still in a coma. Even Tyler has been asking for his daddy and I don't know what to tell him."

Penny put her hand on my shoulder. "We'll figure this out Nikki."

I spent the day working in the shop along with Penny and caught up on some of the bills that had been piling up. I was glad business was still steady cause our savings were dwindling. I made a few more calls to the FBI but was not getting any more information on Dre. I was at my wit's end on what to do. I left the shop at 5:30 to pick Tyler up at the babysitter's and then pop into Wal-Mart on the way home to pick up a few groceries for the house. I pulled into my driveway, got out of the car and then a limo pulled up in front of my house. I knew who it was as soon as I saw it. Bump got out of the driver's side and opened the door for Malachi. He stepped out dressed in a gray two-piece suit and black loafers. He walked over to me by my car and gave me a frown. I returned his frown with one of my own.

"What the hell do you want?" I asked.

"We had an agreement Nikki. You haven't been at the club in three nights. You know what the consequences of breaking our arrangement would mean."

"Things changed." My mind was racing trying to think of what I could say and then it came to me. "You can't hold Dre's life over my head anymore ... he's dead."

A surprised expression came over his face. It was a lie but I didn't want to warn him of the FBI being involved in his relocation.

"Me sorry to hear dat Nikki."

"Whatever. You got exactly what you wanted. My baby's father is dead! Now get the hell out of my life!"

He stared at me blankly as if what I said meant nothing to him. I turned to get Tyler out of the car and he grabbed my arm.

"Get the fuck off me," I yelled.

"Quiet." He spoke with authority. "I normally would have box yuh down for talking to me like dat but I understand yuh're emotional right now so I'll excuse it. Don't get renk wit me."

"You're outta your damn—"

"Shut ya mouth! I don't give a fuck about Dre but yuh … yuh interest me. I've never met a wummon quite like yuh Nikki." He paused and let my arm go. "Regardless of Dre's untimely death we still had an agreement. Dre's debt has been passed onto you and I will still collect."

"Fuck you!"

He gave me a menacing glare and got in my face. "Oh yuh will. Yuh will also be at The Pink Palace this Saturday night ready to work or your son will be growing up in foster care. Your fine ass brings a lot money to the club and I don't plan on losing yuh."

I couldn't believe my ears! "You're fucking crazy!"

He grabbed my throat and it felt like he was choking the shit outta me. Tyler started to cry.

"Don't make me vex Nikki. You will respect me, is dat understood?"

I nodded my head and he let me go. I fell to my knees and tried to catch my breath. This crazy ass nigga would have killed me right in front of my son.

"Good. So I'll see yuh at the club Saturday night. You're a gorgeous woman Nikki and if you behave yourself you'll see what I can do for yuh. I did yuh a favor by getting rid of dat pussyclot, Dre. You'll see what a real man can do for yuh."

I stared up at him with disgust. If I could have, I would've put a bullet between his eyes. He gave me an evil smirk then turned and went back to his limo. Bump opened his door, then got in and drove away. I got up off the ground and opened my car door and consoled Tyler.

"Its okay baby, Mommy is okay," I whispered to him.

I wished that were truth. I was trapped and Malachi

had no intention of letting me be free. I protected Dre but at what cost? Why was he so fucking obsessed with me?

Malachi

I noticed that Nikki didn't show up all weekend so I knew something was up. I hated being so rough with her but her spirit had to be broken before she became my lady. Dre dying was only a bonus. I'd have Dre send Ricky to the hospital to confirm Dre's story and if Dre wasn't dead Ricky would put a bullet in his head. Either way I was done dealing with him. Nikki was the type of chick I could mold into the perfect lady for me. More than that whore Latoya could've ever been.

Things were still uneasy with this mystery nigga, Don P, coming after me. I still had no idea who this nigga was. There was no word on the street on who this pussyhole was or where he came from so I had to take extra precautions and have more security around me at all times. In the meantime I needed to find a new supplier since Jorge had been killed. I made contact with a Cuban named Carlos in Miami who I know worked with some nigga up in New York named King before King got murdered. I had to move fast and reestablish my grip on the Atlanta scene before these other small time pushers decided to move in on my turf.

This Saturday was the annual Hot 107.9 Birthday Bash Concert and it was going to be a big night at the Pink Palace. I need my best dancers in the house cause I had a special appearance by Kane, Beata Douglas and the Flip Set family scheduled to be in the house. Between

Nikki and Jasmine I was going to make a killing! And if this Don P wanted to come after me … I'll be ready for him too.

Chapter Twelve

Just Like Me

Smyrna, GA
Jasmine

Going home was never an easy thing for me. I love my parents but because of my choices in life things were strained with them, especially with my father. They knew about my lifestyle and were very disappointed with my decision. But my mother came to terms with it even though she disapproved. My father barely said two words to me but I didn't care. He liked to sit there and judge me but didn't want to look at skeletons in his own closet. Like the mistress he had for the last twelve years that my mother plays a blind eye to. She busted him having an affair with a teacher at the school he coaches football at. He begged my mother to forgive him for months until she broke down and let him back in her life. I swear she was so weak at times. He swore that it was over but I didn't trust any man. At least I was up front with my life and not lying to anybody about it.

The only reason I visited was because of my mother and her heart condition. She had congestive heart failure three years ago and had a triple bypass. I drove down to Smyrna every two weeks or when I could. Despite all the things we disagreed on, I still loved my mother very much. I made sure if there was anything she needed I bought it for her. I felt like my father resented that I had money like that to spend but that was his problem. I pulled up to the house and used my key to open the front door. I saw my mother sitting on the couch watching Judge Judy.

"Hey Mom."

"Jacqueline!" My mom always called me by my full name. I almost, at times, forget that was my name. "How are you darling?"

She stood up and gave me a hug. "I'm fine Mom, how are you?"

"Oh I'm getting by. Every day is a gift from God."

I have a seat next to her. "That's true. So your breathing has been fine?"

"Yes baby, only when I walk for long distances it becomes a little short but the exercise is still good for me."

"But don't overdo it. I don't want you to end up in the hospital again," I warned her.

"Hush, I'll be fine." She paused then looked at me. "How are you Jacqueline?"

"How do I look?" I leaned back showing off how

good I looked in my BCBG dress and Gucci pumps. "I'm doing great Mom."

"So you're still dancing at that club?" She asked in a disapproving tone.

"Yes I am."

"Why Jacqueline? You're so smart and so beautiful. Why do you sell yourself short? You're a college graduate. You can be doing a number of things instead of that."

I sighed and leaned back, "Like I said plenty of times mother, I'd rather be my own boss making my own money. I'm not just a stripper ... I'm a business. I model; I sell my calendars and posters. I'm independent. I just don't feel like I have to be a part of corporate America to live the American dream."

"So dancing naked in front of perverted men is the American dream? We didn't raise you to be like this Jacqueline."

"No you didn't, I chose this life. I'm happy ... happier than you are being here with Daddy and putting up with his nonsense," I retorted.

My mom sighed. I knew it was a low blow and I regretted throwing it up in her face.

"Don't disrespect your father."

"But he can disrespect you?" I could see the embarrassment on her face. "I'm sorry Mom. I didn't mean that. I just don't wanna have this argument every time I come to see you. I know you don't like my lifestyle but I'm still your daughter and I still love you. I just want you to accept me as I am."

She put her hand on mine, "I love you no matter what Jacqueline. I just want you to be truly happy. Do you ever talk to Rashida and Joyce anymore?"

Rashida and Joyce were my childhood friends I grew up with. I would never admit this to anybody but I systematically destroyed those friendships because of my jealousy of Rashida's relationship. I was in love with her and when she didn't return my feeling, I purposely set out to ruin her relationship with her man. In the process I wrecked our friendship forever. It was one of the few regrets I had that I wished I could change.

"No I don't. I ... really don't wanna talk about them Mom."

"Okay baby." She stared at me. "You do look beautiful even with all that makeup on."

I chuckled, "Thanks Mom."

I spent most of the day with her eating lunch and talking. It felt good being with her. I felt like the regular old Jacqueline Dawson again and not Jasmine the stripper. It was good to get away from it every now and then. I enjoyed spending time with her so much that I forgot what time it was until I heard my dad's truck pull up in the drive way. He came into the house and saw me sitting next to Mom. She got up and greeted him at the door.

"Hello, baby," she gave him a kiss.

He stared at me with those judging eyes, "Jacqueline."

I returned the glare, "Douglas."

Another awkward silence filled the room. He walked by and put his bag down by the couch and walked into the kitchen.

"Well, I guess that's my clue that it's time to go."

"You don't have to leave Jacqueline. This is your home too."

I rolled my eyes, "Not anymore. I gotta get going

anyway. I love you Mom."

"I love you too darling."

I gave her a kiss and bounced. As much as my mom may have wanted my dad and I to be father and daughter again I knew he'd never accept me the way she did. I'd be damned if I put up a front for him. I am who I am and I didn't make any excuses about that.

♛ ♛ ♛ ♛ ♛ ♛ ♛ ♛ ♛ ♛ ♛ ♛ ♛ ♛ ♛ ♛

A couple of days later it was time to get back on my grind. After I did some digging I found out from one of Malachi's boys that the gunfight at Lenox Mall was a hit on him. I guess he wasn't fazed by the attempt on his life. That was a week ago. Today was the Hot 107.9 Birthday Bash so that meant it was gonna be a big night at the Pink Palace. Every celebrity in Atlanta from Jermaine Dupri to Usher was rumored to be coming through the palace doors not to mention the Flip Set Family performing was gonna bring out the niggas with green in their pockets!

The Pink Palace was going to be extra thick and I planned on being the center of attention getting all the money. I went to the Birthday Bash concert at Philips Arena with Kandi and got my drink on enjoying the music but then we left early in order to get dressed for the club. I put on my black teddy and red Steve Madden stilettos and made sure I looked flawless. Kandi put on a new white two-piece bikini I bought her and white platform shoes and was looking like a little sex kitten.

"Damn Jasmine you look fabulous," Kandi crooned.

"I know. You look sexy yourself thanks to my styling

tips." We both laughed. "So are you ready to get this money tonight?"

"Yeah but it looks like she is too," Kandi said and pointed past me.

"Who?"

I turned and I saw Nikki looking in the mirror wearing a sheer black teddy looking like a cross between Meagan Good and Naomi Campbell. I hadn't seen her here in a minute but now she just popped up. I hated to admit it but she looked good. Gorgeous to be more accurate. She had body that was built like a brick house. I walked over to her and Kandi followed behind me.

"Wow ... don't you look sexy," I crooned.

She looked at my reflection in the mirror behind her and rolled her eyes. "What do you want Jasmine?"

"Dang, why you gotta be like that?" She didn't reply but continued to apply her makeup. "So where have you been?"

She turned around, "Listen Jasmine, I'm here to work we don't have to make small talk with each other."

"Fine, just as long as you know who the top bitch is here." She smirked at my words. "You find that shit funny?"

Nikki shook her head. "You just remind me of somebody I knew a few years ago."

I frowned, "I ain't like nobody else baby girl."

"That's just what I used to think," she remarked and walked away.

What the hell was that supposed to mean? I followed her out into the club and watched as Nikki took the main stage. The club was packed with men and women with dollar bills in their hands and it was standing room only. It looked like everybody that was at the concert came to

The Pink Palace to get loose.

Then I heard the DJ announce, "Ladies and Gentlemen, The Flip Set Family is in the house!"

I looked up to the VIP area and saw Kane, Beata Douglas, Ill Tech and their new female rapper called Mocha G. Kane looked so damn fine in his black jeans and his muscular arms in his black Averix shirt. He had an iced out platinum chain around his neck. A gang of dancers and groupies flocked toward the VIP area but security stopped them from entering. I could see why Beata Douglas was hanging on his arm like that ... to keep the hoes away. Beata looked thicker in real life than she did on TV. That Gucci skirt could barely cover all that ass she had. But from what I heard on the gossip sites it was the sexy ass Mocha G she should have been worried about with her half naked self. If she does half the nasty shit she said in her rap lyrics then Beata better watch out.

I turned my eyes toward Malachi's office and saw him staring into the crowd intensely through the bulletproof window of his. There was a lot of security in the club tonight in case anything jumped off. He wasn't taking any chances. The DJ started to play Ludacris, "How Low" and I turned and looked to the center stage.

Nikki began to side step to the beat. She spun around and bent her knees as she slowly dropped to the floor. Then the high pitch vocals of the song came in and she started gyrating her ample ass faster and the crowd went wild. Niggas were throwing money at her left and right! Fuck that. She wasn't gonna outshine me on my own damn stage! I walked to the back and came from behind the pink curtains on stage with Nikki. She looked at me and chuckled. That pissed me off even more. I jumped in front of her and started shaking my ass faster than her making the crowd chant my name. Nikki turned around and got in my face and started to dance just as hard as me. We were straight up battling each other on stage. Then she jumped up and did a suicide split to the floor bouncing her ass on the stage. I refused to be outdone by her. I dropped to a split and start pussy popping right in front of her. The crowd was going crazy and money was falling around us like confetti. The song ended and we stared at each other. Nikki got up, scooped up some bills and walked off stage. She turned and smiled at me again, "Just like me."

Nikki

That damn Jasmine was a trip. I couldn't believe how much like her I was. She thought I was here to take her spot but that wasn't even close to the truth. Malachi was forcing me to be here. It wasn't even about the money anymore … he just wanted me. He was a sick bastard. I had to figure a way out from underneath his thumb.

The Pink Palace was thick tonight. I hadn't seen so many people up in here even in my heyday. Birthday Bash's really packed the people in. Almost every girl was dancing on the stages or doing a lap dance for a dude or a woman. They only let a few girls up in VIP to dance for the rappers. I wondered if Jermaine Dupri was up there? He used to pop up in here on the regular back in the day.

I was the only dancer who was not out front shaking her ass for some money. I was backstage trying to get my mind right. Actually, I needed a drink. As I was standing backstage contemplating my fucked up predicament, security came by with The Flip Set family behind them. Flip Set ... that name brought back memories of that nigga Damien I used to mess with years ago. His criminal organization was called The Flip Set. They came down from New York and started locking Atlanta drug trafficking down. After Damien flipped out on his boss, King, he went back to New York and from what I heard helped form Flip Set Records with his cousin Rob. Kane was their first act and now he was right in front of me—one of the most famous rappers in the game.

Beata Douglas was right behind him. They all had microphones in their hands preparing to take the stage for a performance. Beata looked up at me and it was weird ... we stared at each other for a second. It wasn't a mean mug or an envious glare, it was like with one look we understood each other. Beata stepped over to the side of the stage I was on, "Are you okay?"

"No ... not yet," I answered honestly.

She stared at me for a second then spoke again, "Then do what you have to do in order to be."

"Thank you."

She nodded her head then walked back over to Kane and the others. My respect for her just went up tenfold. She didn't have to take time away from what she was doing to speak to me. I guess she could sense my misery. The DJ got on the mic.

"Ladies and gentlemen coming all the way from New York City to the Pink Palace! Performing their smash hit "Kiss" from their debut compilation album, *United We Stand*, it's The Flip Set family!"

The music started to play a hypnotic beat and Kane, Beata Douglas, Mocha G and Ill Tech all took the stage.

Beata started to sing a riff then started her verse.

(Beata) Do you wanna kiss me? Baby come and kiss me... Do you wanna kiss me? Baby come and kiss me...

(Kane) She got them thick lips/ them Meagan Good lips/ I love to feel them, every time we kiss/ Like a Rogue kiss/ you draining all my powers/ but I'm feeling superhuman/ cause I can do you for hours/ that ass I got tap/ hit it from the back/ sorry you got hair did/ cuz I'm pulling on that/ you know what you doing/ you ain't foolin'/ got me acting like a fool/ when we be screwin'/ but I ain't even mad/ cause you the baddest chick/ that I've ever had

(Beata) Ooh Baby, come and put them lips on me, Baby, I love it when kissing me, baby, you got my body shaking, it's yours for the taking, come and kiss my G-spot,

(Mocha G) He says I'm too mushy/ but I ain't pushy/ cause behind closed doors he loves to kiss on my pussy/ my mocha is so tight/ he want it all night/ I got him addicted on a chocolate high (ha ha ha) I got them juicy lips/ the ones he love to kiss/ do your thing baby, don't stop get it, get it/ pucker up when you kissing on my breasts/ you know Mocha G is the sexists

(Ill Tech) She know she got a man/ but I got plan/ come creep with me/ and I'll be your lover man/ nobody else exist/ baby when we kiss/ I be lickin' all the spots that he missed/ I can do it fast/ or I can do it slow/ I be switchin' speeds/ when I go down below/ your waist

line/ it's all mine/ make your legs shake/ sending shivers up your spine/ we can take a trip/ to whatever beach ya wish/ But I can make ya wet/ with one kiss

(Beata) Ooh Baby, come and put them lips on me, Baby, I love it when kissing me, baby, you got my body shaking, it's yours for the taking, come and kiss my G-spot

They just tore up the stage with that song and the crowd went wild. They were some real talented people. As I looked at how the crowd reacted to their music I saw a familiar face in the back of the club. It was Polo sitting at a table with Malachi's ugly ass brother Reggie and his nigga Chaz. What the hell? I knew he did business with them but he was also hanging out with these muthafuckas too? I walked through the crowd ignoring a few men asking me for a private dance until I reached their table.

"I guess you're a regular here these days," I said sarcastically to Polo.

He looked up at me. "Nikki?"

"Damn girl ... you thick as a muthafucka," Reggie droned.

I ignored his ugly ass. Polo got up from the table and came closer to me.

"Nikki, what are you still doing working here?"

"I can ask you the same question."

Polo sighed then gestured for me to follow him to a quieter area near the restrooms away from Reggie's ears. Polo stared at me seriously, "I told you Nikki that being here is not safe. You should be home with your son."

"If I would I could." I turned up the corner of my lips in disgust. "So you're still here doing business with the niggas that shot your best friend? What kind of shit is that?"

Polo shook his head, "Things are not what you think. Why are you back here dancing again? Is Malachi forcing you?"

"What do you think? He was making me dance here for him!"

Polo frowned and looked up toward Malachi's office, "Muthafucka," he mumbled to himself. "You have to get out of here Nikki it's not safe."

"Why do you keep on saying that? What's going on?"

A guy walked out of the restroom and stared at me and licked his lips. Polo pulled me closer and put his hands on my waist and whispered in my ear, "Niggas are gunning for Malachi. They just tried to kill him in Lenox Mall a week ago."

I smiled, "Well isn't that great news? That will solve my problems," I whispered back to him. "Who's coming after him?"

"I don't know, but I don't want you to get caught in the crossfire. I don't want anything to happen to you." He gazed in my eyes and I saw that he cared for me a lot more than just a friend. His lips were inches away from mine. "I can't have anything happen to you. I'm going to take you home."

"Polo … I can't. Malachi will kill me if I don't dance here," I looked around to make sure nobody was watching us. "I have to go."

"Nikki …"

I pulled away from him, "I have to go."

I walked away from Polo and headed back to the stage. I had no idea he felt so strongly about me. I guess being Dre's best friend he couldn't express himself like that. But what if I never saw Dre again? Should I have told him about the FBI? No, cause I didn't know why he was still doing business with Malachi's crew. I didn't know if I could trust him. But if what he said was true about niggas gunning for Malachi then I hoped they killed his ass.

Chapter Thirteen

Revelations

Atlanta, GA
Jasmine

I ended up making a little over $6,000 the other night at the Birthday Bash night at The Pink Palace. Not bad for one night of work. The only down side was Nikki. I probably would have made more money if her ass wasn't there getting so much attention on the main stage. I couldn't believe I let her get under my skin, but the weird thing about it was, she acted like she really didn't want to be there. So what did Malachi have on her?

I knew curiosity killed the cat but I couldn't help but wonder. Malachi called me up to his office so he probably wanted some ass and as long as he continued to hit me off for my service that was cool with me. Security at the Palace was still deeper than a muthafucka as I went up the stairs to his office. Bump opened the door for me and I saw Malachi on the phone screaming at his workers.

"I don't want fucking excuses! Just find out who this Don P is," he growled. Then he ended the call and tossed his cell on his desk.

"Are you okay baby?" I said.

He looked at me and then grinned, "Don't you worry about it sweet Jasmine. I have other concerns for you."

I raised my eyebrow, "Other concerns? Like what?"

"My dumb ass brother's birthday is this Sunday night and I need you and some of the girls to put on a show for him." I frowned, he smiled, and continued. "Just show him a good time and I'll make sure you'll be well compensated for your services. This is going to be a closed door event so ask a couple of other girls to join you."

"As much as I like to make you feel good Daddy, I'm gonna have to decline the offer. I really don't like him."

Malachi chuckled, "I told him you would say no. Are you sure you don't wanna make some extra cash?"

"I'll pass but I'm sure Hester or Jade will jump on it."

"As you wish."

I walked around his desk and sat in his lap. "Now are there any extra services I can do for you?" I purred in his ear as I felt his hard dick press on my ass in his pants.

"Always," he droned as he unzipped his slacks and pulled out his one eyed monster. I slid down to my knees and gave him a deep oral massage.

‎👑 ‎👑 ‎👑 ‎👑 ‎👑 ‎👑 ‎👑 ‎👑 ‎👑 ‎👑 ‎👑 ‎👑 ‎👑 ‎👑 ‎👑 ‎👑

After I was done servicing Malachi, I went back downstairs and saw Nikki coming in to work. Maybe I had been going about this all wrong. I assumed Malachi brought her in to take my place but I may have jumped the gun a bit. She walked back to the locker room and started to get undressed and I followed her. She peeped my reflection in the mirror behind her and shook her head.

"Hey Nikki."

She simply gave me a head nod.

"Listen, I know we haven't gotten off on the right foot …"

"We don't have to get off on any foot Jasmine. I'm here to work, not make friends."

"I know, but can I ask you a question?"

She sighed, "What?"

"Why are you here?" She turned and looked at me but didn't respond. "Okay, here's a better question, what does Malachi have over your head?"

Her eyebrow raised, "Why do you wanna know so bad?"

"I'm just curious."

"Listen Jasmine, don't worry about me. If I were you I would try to put as much distance between yourself and Malachi as possible. Whoever is gunning for him isn't gonna care who standing next to him," Nikki warned.

"You mean his beef with Don P? What do you know about it?"

"Nothing much and the less is the better. I gotta get

dressed Jasmine," she said and turned and continued to change. I walked over to my dressing table and sat down. Whoever this Don P was seemed to have Malachi taking extra precautions. Why do I feel like Nikki is more involved in all of this than she's letting on?

Nikki

I don't know why Jasmine was trying so hard to find out my business with Malachi but she needed to stay out of it. I don't trust her or anybody in this club. For all I knew Malachi could've been telling her to keep an eye on me. For that reason alone I kept a razor blade hidden on me at all times just in case a bitch got rowdy. But she did confirm what Polo told me the other night about somebody named Don P who was coming after Malachi. If he put a bullet in Malachi's head, I would be happy as hell.

But what else had been playing in my mind was Polo. It seemed like he wanted to protect me more than anything else. He almost kissed me. I never knew he felt that way for me but with Dre somewhere in FBI protection I couldn't even consider doing anything with him. Just as I was getting ready to go out front and dance on stage Bump stepped to me. That nigga looked like a linebacker for the Falcons with his huge self.

"Malachi wants to see you in his office."

I frowned, "For what?"

"I don't know. C'mon on," he ordered.

I had no choice so I followed him up the stairs to Malachi's office. He opened the door and I walked in. There he was sitting behind his big desk smoking a cigar. I hoped he didn't think I was going to give him some ass. I had something for him if he thought that was going down again.

He exhaled a cloud of gray smoke from his mouth and grinned at me. Then he placed his cigar in his marble ashtray, "Come have a seat Nikki."

I did as he said and sat in the chair. Malachi sat back in his black Ralph Lauren button down suit and continued to puff on his cigar. "I need you to come to a private party Sunday night for my little brother."

"Private party? I don't fuck for cash Malachi," I said firmly.

"No one is asking you to. I just need you to be here at the Palace Sunday night and entertain Reggie."

"And if I don't want to?"

Malachi glared at me, "It's not a request."

"Fine," I got up and turn toward the door.

"Sit. I didn't dismiss you," Malachi told me coldly. I wanted to run but I knew I wouldn't get far. I sat back down. He stood up and walked around his desk and stood behind me. "I sent Ricky to check out your story about Dre being dead." My heart sped up in my chest. Does he know that Dre was in FBI protection? "It turned out you were telling me the truth."

"I have no reason to lie."

"Not anymore," he retorted. He placed his hands on my shoulders and caressed me. "I can't help but think about our wonderful night together. You were magnificent."

I felt so disgusted thinking about him being all over me that night. "If you say so."

"I do. You could be more than just a dancer in my club if you behave. I can make you a queen Nikki.

You need to forget about your past because I am your future."

I pulled away from his touch and stood up, "Can I leave now?"

Malachi grinned but with one blinding motion grabbed me by my arm and pulled me close to him. His other hand slapped and grabbed my ass roughly. I could feel his warm breath on my neck as he whispered in my ear, "I love your spirit Nikki and you may not believe it now but you will be mine." He kissed my neck. "And yes, you can leave now."

He let me go and I backed away from him. I would've spit in his face if I thought I could get away with it; instead I hastily walked past him and out of the door and down the stairs. This stupid muthafucka really thought I was going to be his lady then he must be getting high off of his own supply! Ugly ass muthafucka! Now he got me going to some birthday or fuck party for his stupid brother. Malachi was running my life like it was his to control and there was nothing I could do to stop it. I needed to find a way out of here and out of Malachi's life.

Perhaps I hadn't really explored all my options? Polo. I knew he was still being supplied by Malachi but he doesn't have any love for him either. Maybe there was something he could do. After I get off of working at the Pink Palace I made a phone call to Polo. He picked up on the second ring.

"Who this?" he answered.

"It's me Polo," I replied as I drove down Spring Street toward the highway entrance to I-75 South.

"Nikki. Are you okay?" I could hear the concern in his voice.

"Yeah ... I need to see you."

"Okay, I'm over in Camp Creek right now."

"I can meet you at Chilli's in ten minutes?"

"Cool, I'll see you then."

"Okay," I replied and end the call.

I exit off of I-20 on to I-285 South and head toward Camp Creek on Exit 2. I've known Polo for as long as I've known Dre. The two were inseparable and whatever Dre decided to do Polo was always right there by his side. The only thing Polo didn't do was get out of the drug game when Dre did. Even though Dre encouraged him to leave it alone, he also understood that Polo was a grown man and the game and fast money could be addictive. It must've been during that time Polo started getting his supply directly from Malachi.

I pulled into the Camp Creek Market Place and into the parking lot of Chilli's and parked. I got out and went inside where the hostess greeted me. I then spotted Polo at a booth near the bar and made my way over to him and had a seat.

"Hey Nikki, you look good."

I smiled, "Thanks."

"I ordered some wings for us already. What you drinking?"

"A Blue Margarita would be nice," I replied.

Once the waitress came over with the wings Polo placed my drink order. I started to munch on the hot wings and didn't realize how hungry I was until I was on my fifth wing.

"I'm sorry Polo, I'm just eating all your wings ..."

He smiled, "Don't worry about it."

The waitress came with my drink and another beer for Polo.

"I heard about Dre passing away." Polo paused then gazed in my eyes. "I'm so sorry Nikki."

I wished I could have told him the truth but the less he knew about Dre's whereabouts with the FBI the better off he'd be. "It's not your fault Polo. Malachi is to blame for all of this."

"So what's going on Nikki? After our talk the other night I didn't think you wanted to see me again."

I took a sip of my drink. "Polo, I don't know who's watching me in the club. I didn't want you to get in trouble for being seen with me. Besides I don't know who I can trust."

"Don't worry about me. You sounded kinda distressed over the phone. Is Malachi making you—"

"No ... not yet," I cut him off.

Polo frowned. "I don't want you going back there Nikki. I can take you out of town until things get settled with Malachi."

His offer sounded good but I couldn't leave town yet without knowing where Dre was. "No, I ... I have too much invested here in Atlanta. Friends, family, a business, and Tyler. Besides Malachi would only try and track me down or worse, go after my family here." I took another gulp of my Margarita. "What do you know about the niggas coming after Malachi?"

Polo took a sip of his beer, "I know they got that nigga Malachi scared shitless. It's just a matter of time before they get his ass," Polo said with a smile on his face.

"I heard that it's somebody named Don P coming after him. Have you ever heard of him?"

"Naw, never heard of him," he said, still grinning.

I stared at Polo and then it dawned on me and I put

my drink down on the table. "Polo ... are you Don P?" Polo took another sip of his beer. "Oh my God ... Polo. Why didn't you tell me you were going to do this?"

Polo leaned in closer, "Keep your voice down Nikki." He looked around and focused back on me. "I was going to tell you but you kind went off grid. That nigga Malachi was supposed to be already dead by now but after shit went wrong in Lenox Mall he's rolling with almost an army around him."

I was shook. I didn't know Polo was plotting this hostile takeover this whole time. "You were behind that hit at Lenox? My God Polo ... a lot of innocent people got hurt."

"It wasn't supposed to go down like that. The niggas I got to do the job got sloppy and that nigga Malachi is no fool." He took a sip of his beer. "Once he took out the first nigga he was ready for war and was shooting first and asking questions later. Four of the six niggas I sent in didn't make it back."

I finished off my Margarita, "So that's why you've been hanging out at The Pink Palace so much?"

"Yeah, I been getting close to his idiot brother finding out what Malachi's been doing for months now," Polo explained.

I looked at him with amazement, "For months? You've been planning this for months? Did Dre know about this?"

"No. Dre would never let me do this so I had to put this in motion without him. I just never thought Malachi would put a hit on Dre before I could take his ass out."

I felt so bad now. "So that day at the hospital when I called you a coward for not going after Malachi ... you were already planning to do just that. I'm so sorry

Polo."

"Don't worry about it Nikki. I wanted to tell you so bad but I didn't want to put you in danger. But then you started dancing in the club and that's the last thing I wanted to see. How did that happen?"

I leaned back in my seat. "At the time Dre was laid up in the hospital Malachi was sending niggas to check up on his condition. I was afraid he was going to send somebody to finish the job, so I volunteered to do whatever to spare his life and now he's dead and Malachi is holding his debt over my head."

Polo took my hand, "Don't worry Nikki, I'm gonna make sure that nigga is dead if it's the last thing I do." I looked in his eyes and I knew he meant every word. "Nikki, I know you're still hurting from Dre's death but … I'm always going to be here to take care of you. I need to tell you this."

Now I felt so guilty for not telling Polo the truth about Dre being alive. "Polo …"

"I know Nikki, but just hear me out. You were my best friend's lady and I know I'm wrong for feeling like this but I can't help it. I've been in love with you for years Nikki."

"Oh God, Polo you don't love me…"

"But I do. I just couldn't say it because you were Dre's lady so I didn't want to betray him like that. I'm not expecting you to say you feel the same way about me right now but in the next few weeks things are going to change. That nigga Malachi is gonna be dead and I'm going to be the man running these streets."

"Polo … I don't know what to say."

He placed his finger on my lips and stood up. "You don't have to say a word. In the days to come you'll see that everything I'm doing now … I'm doing for us."

Polo kissed me, then he pulled away and took a fifty-dollar bill out of his pocket and put it on the table. "Just keep on making Malachi think you're there for him and give me whatever information you can on his whereabouts. It'll make it easy for me to finish him off."

I stared at Polo still in shock, "Okay."

"I'll be in touch Nikki."

He walked away and I felt so guilty like I was leading him on. I couldn't tell him Dre was still alive. Not after all he said to me. Polo orchestrated this whole takeover of Malachi and was my only way to deal with him for good. I couldn't have said anything to him right now because he had to stay focused and finish the job on Malachi. But what am I going to do after that?

Chapter Fourteen

Private Party

Atlanta, GA
Nikki

The last two days were a blur since Polo revealed to me everything he had been doing and what he felt for me. I never knew he had been carrying a torch for all these years. I didn't know what was more shocking, the fact that he was in love with me or that he was Don P gunning for Malachi. I never would have suspected that he had been masterminding the whole take over by himself. I mean Polo was not stupid. But running game on this level? I never would have thought. I had to keep the fact that Dre was still alive a secret until this was over.

It was Sunday night and Malachi was throwing a private party for his brother. Now back in my day I fucked with niggas a lot more unattractive than Reggie but there was something about this little foul nigga I just didn't like. Maybe it was the way he was always harassing the other dancers, the lustful looks he always gave me, or maybe because he was Malachi's brother but he really turned me off.

The Pink Palace was closed to the general public by six o'clock and by eight o'clock a bunch of Reggie's friends and street niggas came in. Malachi wasn't at the club and that was a relief. I didn't have to look at his ass. A few other girls were already giving niggas dances and I spotted a couple of girls getting fucked in the private VIP rooms. Back in the day that would have been me tricking up in that room for the right amount of cash, but them days were long gone for me. I was hoping to see Polo tonight but I guess he didn't make the guest list. Reggie was dressed in black jeans and a long sleeved tee shirt with three platinum chains around his neck acting like he was a don or some shit. With Malachi gone I guess he thought he was heir to the throne.

Reggie jumped up with a bottle of Nuvo in his hands, "Listen here niggas! All these bitches here tonight are here for your entertainment! But I get the first lap dance from all of them hoes!"

Straight retard. The idiot and his boys got pissy drunk for the next couple of hours. I spent most of my time hanging with Gina at the bar avoiding the horny niggas trying to rub on my ass. I looked and saw Kandi, Jasmine's home girl with Hester and Jade sitting at a table with some of Reggie's niggas, Chaz and them, snorting cocaine. Damn, I could tell she was being sucked into the lifestyle and she was not going to last long at this rate. When I first brought Mo'Nique into The Pink Palace back in the day I kept her clear of shit like that. Jasmine was not even here so I knew if she knew what Kandi was doing, she would object. I would say something but it wasn't my place. I was just here to do a job so that was what I was going to do and get the hell up outta Dodge!

Reggie took to the stage and sat on a chair facing the main curtain. The DJ started to play Ying Yang Twins' "The Whisper Song" and I strutted out from behind the curtain dressed in a black two-piece thong and bra set and black Gucci pumps. Reggie's eyes bugged out of his head when he saw my thickness. I seductively wound my body matching the rhythm of the song, "Like B-AM, B-AM, B-AM, B-AM, B-AM, B-AM, B-AM, B-AM ..."

I grabbed the pole, swung around and landed like a black panther on the prowl. I crawled my way over to Reggie in the chair and climbed up on him.

"Oh shit," Reggie uttered to me softly and felt on my titties. I turned around and sat on his lap and grinded my ass in his crotch making his manhood stand to attention. I bent over and placed my hands on the stage floor in front of me and put my fat ass in Reggie's face and made my ass cheeks talk to him. The men in the club all shouted and made catcalls at me. I rolled away from Reggie as the song ended and I danced my way back across the stage and disappeared behind the curtain. Like always, I left them wanting more. I headed to the empty locker room to change and get the fuck out. I took off my bra and dropped it in my bag. When I looked up I saw Reggie behind me.

"What the fuck you doing in here nigga?"

He grinned and looked at my titties then grabbed my right breast, "I'm here to finish our dance."

I slapped his hand away, "Get the fuck off me nigga! I ain't one these easy hoes you fuck with!"

I guess he didn't like that because he rushed me and grabbed me by the neck and hemmed me up on my dressing table. "Bitch you gonna give me this pussy! It's my fucking birthday so I get it my way!"

He was already positioned in between my legs and he reached down and ripped my thongs off exposing my pussy. Then he struggled to get his dick out of his pants. I had been raped before and it was the most demeaning and disgusting thing ever done to me. Memories of the beating and rape flashed back to me like it was yesterday. It took me a long time to get over that whole ordeal. I promised myself I would never let another nigga violate me like that again. Unluckily for Reggie I was able to get my hands on the razor blade I had on top of my dressing table and I grabbed it. Suddenly he froze as he felt a sharp prick on his neck.

"What the—"

"Shut the fuck up," I yelled. I had half a thought to slit his throat from ear to ear but he was lucky he was Malachi's brother or he'd be bleeding on the floor right now. "Get your fucking hands off me!"

He quickly raised his hands as if he surrendered. "Whoa, listen Nikki … don't …"

"I said shut the fuck up," I roared and pressed the blade harder against his skin.

"Aaaahhhh … Okay, okay," he yelped.

A stream of blood trickled down his neck. His eyes became wide as saucers as he looked at me with fear. I pushed him back off me, "If you ever put your fucking hands on me again … I will kill you. Understand?"

"Yeah … okay!"

"Get the fuck out!" I mushed him in the head and he staggered back and grabbed his neck. I held the razor in my hand ready to slice him open if he tried me again but the little bitch didn't want none. He slowly backed away from me and left the locker room. He didn't know how close he was to losing his life on his birthday. I waited a minute before I put the blade down then quickly got dressed into my street clothes and exited the club through the back. As I was walking to my car I saw three niggas walking with Kandi to a car and putting her in the back seat. She looked completely fucked up, high as a bird. She could barely keep her eyes open. I knew this was not a good look so I rushed over to them.

"Hey! Where do you think you're taking her?" I yelled. One of the niggas named Chaz, who was part of Reggie's crew, mean mugged me.

"What the fuck does it matter to you?"

I took a step closer. "Let her out of the car now!"

"Get the fuck outta here bitch," Chaz barked at me.

"C'mon man, let's get outta here," another nigga yelled at Chaz.

"Kandi! Kandi get out of the car!" I yelled at her but she could barely look at me. She laughed and leaned her head against the nigga next to her in the back seat. Chaz started the engine and mashed down on the gas. I jumped out of the way at the last second before he ran me over. I rushed back inside of the club and went over to Gina, the bartender.

"Gina, do you have Jasmine's phone number?"

"Yeah, what's up?"

"I need to her call now!"

Jasmine

The melodic sounds of Monica's "Everything To Me" resonated from my cell waking me up from my sleep. I looked at the display and saw a 404 number I didn't recognize so I ignored it and rested my head back on my pillow. One minute later the phone rang again and it was the same number. I didn't like answering numbers I didn't know but if this fucker kept on calling back I would never get any sleep.

I answered, "Who is this?"

"Jasmine it's me Nikki."

I sat up in bed. "Nikki? How did you get my number?"

"Gina gave it to me. Listen, your girl Kandi is in trouble."

I rubbed my eyes, "What are you talking about? What trouble?"

"She was here at Reggie's party getting fucked up."

My eyebrows crinkled, "Reggie's party? I told her not to go—"

"Listen to me Jasmine, Kandi left here with Chaz and two other niggas and she is high as hell!"

Fear shot through my body. "Oh shit!"

"You need to get here cause them niggas looked like they was gonna run a train on her ass."

"Oh my God … I'll be there in fifteen minutes."

"Okay."

I ended the call, jumped up out of bed and threw on my pink Baby Phat sweat suit and pulled my hair back into a ponytail. One minute later I was in my car headed toward The Pink Palace. I couldn't believe Kandi went to that damn party after I told her ass not to fuck with them! I didn't know why I even cared so much about what happened to Kandi but a part of me felt responsible for her. She was so damn naïve. I raced down Peachtree Road toward the club and finally pulled into the parking lot and I saw Nikki and Gina waiting for me.

I jumped out of my Benz, "What the hell is going on?"

"Like I said Jasmine your girl Kandi got in a car with Chaz and two other niggas and took off. She was totally fucked up," Nikki explained to me.

"Who was she here with?"

"She was getting high with Hester and Jade all night," Gina informed me.

I cut my eyes to the club entrance. "Them bitches!"

I stormed toward the club and Nikki and Gina were right behind me. When I got inside I looked around and saw niggas still partying. Reggie was in a booth holding a napkin to his neck for some reason. Then I spotted them two scandalous hoes Hester and Jade giving lap dances to some niggas.

I marched over to the Filipino bitch Hester, "You stupid bitch! Why did you let her go with Chaz and 'em!?"

Hester flipped her long black hair and looked me up and down. "What the fuck you talking about bitch?"

"Kandi! You dumb bitches got her high and then let that grimy ass nigga Chaz take her outta here," I roared. My loud voice began to draw a few stares from the people around us but I didn't give a damn. Reggie and a couple of his niggas started to walk over to us but then I saw Nikki ice grillin' him then took her finger and made a cut throat gesture across her neck. Reggie apparently knew what that meant and motioned for his niggas to go sit back down.

"I ain't her momma. She a grown ass woman. If she wanna go make some paper then that's her business," Hester retorted.

"But you knew she was fucked up and you still let her go. Why weren't you looking out for her?"

"Bitch, ain't that yo job? What? You afraid Chaz is gonna stretch out that little tight pussy of hers? I know you like that coochie nice and tight Jasmine," Hester said in a sarcastic tone then licked her tongue between two of her fingers.

Both Hester and Jade started laughing but I snapped. I grabbed Hester by her long hair and pulled her up out of the lap of the dude she was dancing for and pulled her head back.

"Owwww," she yelled.

"You listen to me bitch, if anything happens to Kandi I'ma come back and whoop your ass!"

I gave her hair another tug pulling her head back further. She always bragged about having real hair on her head. Guess the bitch wasn't lying cause I was about to rip her shit off her scalp. I pushed her ass forward, back into the lap of the dude she was dancing for, and she grabbed her head. Then I stepped to Jade who was still sitting in the other dude's lap and I pimp slapped her ass across the face. I was so pissed I wished she would have tried to fight back so I could break my foot off in her ass. But none of them wanted none of what I had. I turned and walked away and Nikki was right behind me.

"Where are you going?" she asked.

"I know Chaz hustles out in Bankhead so that's where I'm going."

We both exit out the back of the Pink Palace and walked over to my car. Nikki walked around to the passenger side. "What are you doing?"

Nikki looked at me, "I'm coming with you."

"You don't have to do that."

"I know, but I wanna see this through to the end," she said sincerely.

I nodded my head in understanding. We both got into my car and I pulled out of the parking lot and headed to Bankhead. What the hell was Kandi thinking? I wanted to blame her but I saw what she was doing with Hester and Jade and I didn't try harder to stop her. Hester called her a grown ass woman but Kandi was far from grown. In all actuality she was still very much a little girl. I should've encouraged her to work things out with her boyfriend and get the hell out of the lifestyle, but instead I decided to be her guru and pulled her in deeper. I even seduced her for the hell of it. The more I thought about it I didn't even know her real name. What the hell was I thinking?

"This is not your fault you know," Nikki mentioned to me as we drove on the highway. "I know you think it is but it's not."

"It is. I should have seen this coming."

Nikki looked at me, "How could you?" I didn't have an answer. "I've been where you are right now."

"You don't have to say that to make me feel better."

"I'm not. A few years ago I got my little cousin caught up dancing at The Pink Palace. I schooled her on the do's and don'ts of the game and because of me she got caught up in some real life and death shit. I should have never brought her into this game. I was lucky she got out of this lifestyle before it ruined her," Nikki confessed.

I glanced over to her, "Why did you get out? You could be running this shit by now."

She chuckled, "That's what I thought, but we both know in reality, as long as you're the one swinging on the pole you're never gonna run this shit."

We rode in silence for a few minutes and her words really resonated with me. I guess she really was me a few years ago. So where did I go from here?

"What kind of car was Chaz driving?"

"A gray Dodge Charger. Have you tried calling her?" she asked.

"No … shit. I should've been tried that." I took out my cell and speed dialed Kandi's number. After six rings her voicemail picked up. "She's not answering."

We soon exited off I-20 and drove down Lee Street. I really didn't fuck with this side of town if I didn't have to. Nikki seemed to know this area like the back of her hand as she navigated me through the hood like a ghetto tour guide. This was the area that Chaz hustled in and we drove to a few motels but didn't spot his car. An hour or so passed and still no luck. The more time that passed the more my concern for Kandi's safety grew. We really didn't know where Chaz could have taken her.

"We're wasting our time … there's no telling where they could be," I said to Nikki.

"We have to do something. What do you know about this nigga Chaz?"

"I know he's an asshole. He runs the streets with Reggie and he's almost as perverted as him. He's just another one of these young wannabe thugs who thinks he's the man."

"Typical," Nikki quipped.

"I just don't want anything to happen to her. I don't--"

My cell started to sing Monica's "Everything To Me." I looked at the display and Kandi's name illuminated. I quickly answered. "Kandi! Where are you?"

"Jasmine ... please come ... get me."

I pulled my car into the parking lot of a Texaco gas station/Hood Mart and parked. "Are you okay?" I asked frantically.

"Please ... just come and get me..." she responded weakly.

"Okay baby, I just need to know where you are," I said as calmly as I could.

"I don't know ..."

Nikki touched my arm. "What did she say?"

"She doesn't know where she is," I answered. "Kandi, I need you to look outside and tell me what you see."

"Okay." I heard her struggling to move around and it sounded like she fell off of a bed. "Kandi!"

She didn't respond but I heard her still moving. "The ... Super 8 ..." she mumbled.

"The Super 8." I turned and looked at Nikki, "Where the hell is that?"

"College Park off of Old National. C'mon lets get back on 285 South."

I pulled out of the Texaco lot and headed toward the highway. I tried to keep Kandi talking but after a second or two she wasn't responding anymore and my heart sunk into my gut. I prayed that she still alive. Within a few minutes we exited onto Old National Highway and we pulled up to The Super 8. After describing to the night manager who we were looking for she remembered her and took us to the second floor and opened room 214. When the door opened, I couldn't stop the tears from flowing down my face. Kandi was lying on the floor, buck naked, looking like a broken doll with blood between her legs. The odor in the room was a pungent funk of pussy and dick. The mattress had blood all over it. I rushed to Kandi's side and by the grace of God she was still breathing. Nikki got on her cell and called 911.

Chapter Fifteen

Preexisting Condition

East Point, GA
Nikki

What a hell of a night. If you would had told me I would have been sitting in a cold ass waiting room in South Fulton Hospital with Jasmine I would have laughed. The whole situation hit so close to home for me. I was raped and beaten like a dog by a nigga named Damien. Seeing Kandi nearly in the same condition in the motel room. sprawled out on the floor, naked, with blood between her legs, gave me flashbacks of what happened to me. That sent a chill up my spine.

Jasmine was in tears and in shock seeing Kandi like that. No doubt blaming herself for what happened to her. She rode in the ambulance with Kandi while I followed behind them in Jasmine's Benz. In the short time I had known Jasmine I had never seen her like this. She reminded me so much of myself a few years ago; a money hungry bitch using her body to get what she wanted. The reflection of myself was scary to look at, but I guess seeing Kandi broke down all of Jasmine's defenses and her ho-ology mindframe. We were lucky Kandi carried her I.D. and surprisingly a Humana insurance card in her purse. Her real name was Candice Ford, 19 years old.

"She's going to be okay Jasmine."

Jasmine looked at me sitting next to her in the chair, "Thank you for calling and telling me what happened to her. I ... I haven't exactly been the nicest person to you."

I chuckled. "It comes with the job description; show no love to the competition in the club."

She laughed too. "Who said you were competition for me?"

"See, you're already feeling better."

She looked at the floor. "I should have done better by her. I should have kept a closer eye on her. Made sure she didn't get caught up with them nasty bitches up in there."

"You could've done all that and this still could have happened. She made a bad decision, but she's lucky to have a friend like you," I consoled her.

"A friend like me?" Jasmine shook her head. "That's a joke. I could've been a lot better."

"Then be that now."

She smiled at me. "I can do that."

We sat in silence for a few minutes. We didn't notice it at first because we were so concerned with Kandi's condition but we were gaining a few stares from some men in the emergency waiting room. All kinds of weirdos were up in here at this time of night.

Jasmine was wearing a form fitting pink Baby Phat sweat suit that hugged her voluptuous body and I doubted that she had any panties on underneath. I did wake her up out of her sleep. I had just left The Pink Palace and was dressed in my True Religion jeans and a tight black Hello Kitty tee shirt that snuggled my breasts. A dude got up from his chair and walked over to us. He just stopped and stared at us like we were a pair of steaks on the grill.

Jasmine looked at me and then we both looked at him. "What the hell are you staring at?"

"Yeah, put your fucking tongue back in your mouth and keep it moving," Jasmine snapped. The dude got an embarrassed expression on his face and went and sat back down.

"Niggas!" Jasmine shook his head. "Even when they're hurt they dicks still control their brains."

"Typical. We're not even on the clock," I quipped.

"Speaking of which, what's up with you and Reggie?" Jasmine inquired.

I frowned. "That asshole."

"Yeah that asshole. I saw the gesture you gave him. What was up with that?"

"That little nigga thought just because I gave him a dance for his birthday that he was gonna get some ass too."

Jasmine frowned. "I hate that little ugly muthafucka. I always gotta stop him from harassing the new girls."

"Well, that nigga came back into the locker room while I was changing and tried to take some pussy. So I grabbed my razor blade and put it to his neck. He's lucky his ass is Malachi's brother or he would be dead right now," I told her.

"You should've slit his throat! I swear when I catch up to Chaz and them I'm going to castrate them fuckers," Jasmine said with vengeance.

"I'm with you on that. Niggas like that need to be dealt with severely."

Just then a male nurse, dressed in blue scrubs, with a chart in his hand walked out to us. He was a handsome, light skinned brother who looked a lot like Lenny Kravitz. "Are you friends of Miss Ford?"

Jasmine stood up. "Yes, I'm her sister, is she okay?" she lied so she could find out what was going on with her.

"Yeah she's doing a little better now but she was not in good shape when she came in. We had to pump her stomach. I'm Chauncey Williams and I'll be covering her room tonight."

"She was raped," I said to him.

"Raped?" Chauncey looked at me oddly. "We checked her out and we didn't find any vaginal tearing. We found traces of semen but it didn't appear to be forced sex."

"But there was so much blood," Jasmine told him.

Nurse Chauncey got an embarrassed expression on his face. "Ah … Miss Ford started her menstrual cycle."

"Oh," I said, relieved. Chaz and the others must have bugged out when they saw her bleeding like that and left her there.

"Miss Ford had a lot of drugs in her system though. Cocaine, ecstasy and alcohol. Someone with her condition should really not be doing those types of things," Nurse Chauncey stressed.

Jasmine looked at him oddly. "With her condition?"

"Yeah … Miss Ford has an enlarged heart. Her heart rate was unusually slow so we ran an Echo on her and discover the defect."

Jasmine exhaled deeply and shook her head, "Is she going to be okay?"

"Yes, luckily … if you can call this happening lucky you two brought her in and we can start treating her now. If she had never come in she could have had a heart attack at almost anytime," Nurse Chauncey explained. "Do you wanna see her?"

"Yes, thank you," Jasmine and I followed Chauncey back through the double doors to one of the rooms. We saw Kandi lying in bed with all kinds of tubes going up her nose, arm and chest running to machines, beeping and monitoring her condition. Her face was puffy as she laid under a thin bed sheet.

"I'll give y'all some time," Chauncey said as he closed

the door behind him.

Kandi opened her eyes and saw us standing next to her bed.

"Hey Kandi, you feel better?" Jasmine asked.

Kandi nodded her head, "Yeah ... I fucked up huh?"

Jasmine took her hand, "Don't worry about that. Just concentrate on getting better."

"Hey Kandi," I said and touched her leg.

"Hey Nikki ... I'm sorry... I didn't listen to you."

"You weren't thinking straight. Did Chaz and them hurt you?" I asked trying to make sure.

"I ... don't really remember too much of what happened but ... I think I came on my period and grossed them out," Kandi explained.

"Don't worry about them. So how come you never told me about ..."

"My heart," Kandi finished Jasmine's sentence.

"Yeah, you should've told me."

Kandi shrugged her shoulders, "Didn't think you wanted to hear about that."

Jasmine took her hand, "I do now."

Jasmine

Both Nikki and I sat with Kandi until she dozed off to sleep hours later. The poor girl was really messed up. I decided to give Nikki a ride back to The Pink Palace to pick up her car. I was so glad she was here with me cause I was so fucked up in my heart when we found Kandi in that motel room. I didn't think it would hit me this hard.

"Thank you for staying with me at hospital Nikki," I said to her as I drove down the street.

"It wasn't a problem."

"Listen, whatever Malachi is holding over your head find a way to get out of it because once he's got a grip on you ...

he won't let go."

I pulled into the parking lot of The Pink Palace next to Nikki's black Cutlass Deville.

Nikki stared at me. "I know. I'm working on something. What are you going to do about Kandi?"

"I'm going to help her. She needs somebody … she needs a friend."

"Good, I guess I'll see you Wednesday night?"

"Yeah, I'll see you then." Nikki opened the car door, "Wait."

Nikki stopped and looked at me, "Do you still have my number in your phone?"

She nodded, "Yeah."

"Well, if you need any help dealing with anything, call me."

Nikki nodded and got out of my car and into hers. After what Nikki did for me tonight I felt like I owed her one. I pulled off and headed back to the hospital. I stopped by the gift shop downstairs and bought Kandi some flowers then went up to the fourth floor to her room. When I went in I saw that she just finished breakfast and Nurse Chauncey was checking her vitals.

"How you feeling?"

Kandi frowned, "Like I had my stomach pumped. Now they are forcing me to eat this nasty food."

"It's not that bad Candice," Chauncey interjected.

I smiled, "Eat up."

"Well, your sister is doing much better Jasmine," Chauncey said in a sarcastic tone letting me know he knew I was lying.

I grinned, "Thanks."

He turned and looked at Kandi, "Try and get some rest. I'll be back a little later with Dr. Adams and we're going to run a few more tests."

"Okay."

"I'll see ya later ladies," Chauncey said and walked out

of the room. I took a seat in the chair next to her bed.

"You told him you were my sister?" Kandi asked.

"Yeah … guess he let me slide with that one."

"He's cute," Kandi noted.

I nodded in agreement. "Yeah. Anyway, how do you feel?"

Kandi looked away from me, "Like a fool. I know you're disappointed with me."

"I'm more disappointed with myself than you."

She got a confused expression. "Why? You weren't the one who got fucked up and taken to a motel by a bunch of niggas."

"No but I should've been more of a friend to you. I saw the road you were heading down fucking with Hester and Jade and I should've stopped you then."

Kandi shook her head, "I should've listened to you."

We sat in silence for a moment and I listened to the beep of the hospital equipment monitoring Kandi's heart. "So how long have you known about your heart condition?"

"For about seven years now," she told me.

"So that's why you had an insurance card in your purse?"

"Yeah."

I frowned, "You shouldn't have been dancing at the club then."

"It's okay. I'm supposed to engage in regular exercise on a weekly basis anyway. It's good for me. It keeps my heart strong."

"Ok, so cocaine and ecstasy keeps your heart strong too?" I asked in a motherly tone. Kandi didn't respond. "Well, that shit ends today. You hear me?"

She looked at me with them big brown eyes of hers. "Yeah Jasmine?"

"And so does your dancing at The Pink Palace."

Kandi sat up and looked at me and shook her head. "I can't do that Jasmine. That's how I'm paying my rent. I'm already a month behind on it as it is."

My eyebrows raised, "How come you're so behind?"

"Well," Kandi exhaled and rested her head back on her pillow. "When Rayshawn broke up with me he left me in the apartment stuck with the rent and all the other bills we had coming in."

"Where are your parents?"

"Florida," she replied. "They think I'm still a student at Clark Atlanta."

"What happened?"

Kandi looked at me. "Well, I'm from St. Petersburg. I got a scholarship to go to Clark and I fucked up. I partied my ass right out of it. My grades slipped and never got back up so I lost my scholarship. My folks don't know that. But I had a plan, that's why I started dancing at the Pink Palace and paying my tuition out of pocket. I moved in with Rayshawn and I had it under control until he left me hanging. Pretty soon I couldn't keep up and I dropped outta school."

Damn, that's what I did when I was in college except I was making so much money dancing that after I graduated I just kept on dancing because the money was good. I made myself a business. Kandi wasn't so lucky.

I thought to myself for a second then took her hand. "Okay Kandi, this is what we're going to do. When you get out of here you're going to move you and your stuff into my condo in Buckhead. Then we're going to get you healthy again and you're going to get your ass back in school," I informed her.

Kandi had a dumbfounded expression on her face, "Jasmine ... I ... why are you doing all this?"

"Because," I smiled. "You deserve more out of life than this."

Kandi smiled with joy. "I ... don't know what to say."

"Just say you'll try to do better."

"I will." Kandi paused and then looked at me. "Jasmine don't take this the wrong way, but what happened between us back at Young Reezy's house party ..."

I held up my hand. "We had fun that night but that is not what this is about. You'll have your own room and you're free to see whoever you want." Kandi smiled. "Now if you come in drunk one night and climb in my bed you just might be asking for it."

We both laughed. "Jasmine can I ask you something?"

"Sure what is it?"

"What's your real name? I mean all this time we've known each other I've never asked you that."

I grinned, "Well, Candice. My name is Jacqueline Dawson but only my mother calls me that."

"I like that. Your mother lives around here?"

"Smyrna. She and my father live out there."

"You still talk to them?" she asked.

"My mother yeah. My father doesn't approve of my lifestyle so we haven't talked in years really. I could care less about him." I rolled my eyes.

"Oh, my folks would die if they knew I've been dancing." She paused and looked at me. "Am I asking you too many questions now?"

"No." I shook my head. "Can I tell you something?"

Kandi's eyebrows rose, "Yeah, of course."

"My mother suffered from congestive heart failure. So when I found out about your condition it really hit home. Scared the hell outta me actually."

Kandi got a sad expression on her face "I'm sorry Jasmine." She reached over and hugged me. Feeling her sincere embrace made me realize how much I needed it.

"It's okay Kandi. Now let's get you better okay?"

Kandi smiled, "Okay."

Chapter Sixteen

Holding Back the Years

College Park, GA
Nikki

Penny kept Tyler last night and that was a blessing. I hated to admit but I've kept my distance from Janelle so she didn't get involved in this shit again. After seeing Kandi laid up in the hospital, my decision to keep my distance was the right one. There was no way I was going to drag her into this mess again. I picked up Tyler, dropped him off at day care then headed home. As soon as I got settled into my bedroom my head hit the pillow and I was out.

👑 👑 👑 👑 👑 👑 👑 👑 👑 👑 👑 👑 👑 👑 👑 👑

About six hours later my phone woke me up out of a deep sleep. Polo's name was on display. I wondered if he had anything new to tell me.

I accepted his call. "What's up Polo?"

"Nothing much, I was in your part of town and wanted to see you. Are you home?"

"Yeah," I sat up in bed. "Come on over."

"Okay, I'll be there in fifteen minutes."

"Cool, see you then." I ended the call.

I got up, went in the shower and freshened up. Five minutes later I got out of the shower, threw on a blue summer dress then went into the kitchen and warmed up some left over pasta. I hadn't eaten anything since yesterday. After I got a few bites in I heard my doorbell. Quickly clearing my mess, I walked to the front door and opened it. Polo stood before me, of course wearing a red Polo shirt, some Ecko Unlimited jeans with a Gucci belt and a pair of matching Gucci printed Nikes.

"Hey Polo," I greeted, and he came in.

Polo looked at me with a concerned expression on his face, "What's going on Nikki? I heard some shit went down at Reggie's birthday party last night."

I wondered if Reggie told him about what I did to him. "What they saying?"

"They saying you and Jasmine rolled up on some bitches and regulated they ass. What was that all about?" Polo took a seat on the couch.

I guess Reggie decided to keep our little encounter to himself. "Yeah we did. Some foul shit went down with another one of the girls, Kandi, that Hester and Jade could've stopped but didn't. Long story short, Chaz and two other niggas took advantage of the girl and left her in a bad predicament last night."

"Chaz? That stupid muthafucka that be with Reggie all the time?" Polo asked and shook his head in disbelief. "Figures. Is she all right?"

I sat on the couch next to Polo, "She's at South Fulton but not really in that good of shape but not because of what they did. She has some other medical issues."

"That's fucked up but I'm glad everything is straight now." Polo looked into my eyes. "I wanted to see you again. You've been on my mind like crazy these past couple of days."

Damn, I almost forgot that he said that he loved me the other night. Or maybe I just didn't want to remember it. And here I was, in this little dress fresh out the shower, and he was looking at me like a scoop of chocolate ice cream on a sugar cone.

I exhaled and looked at him seriously, "Polo ... I'm not sure we should ..."

He leaned over and kissed me. I had to admit he was a damn good kisser. His hand touched my bare thigh and I felt my pussy jump. It had been a minute since I was intimate with anybody I was attracted to. The last man I was with was Malachi and that was torture. He made my skin crawl. The last man that made me feel good was Dre. The man I love. Polo's lips tugged at mine with a passion I never knew he had for me. His hand started to move up my thigh but I stopped him from going further. I pulled away from his lips slowly. Dre was still alive and I was still very much in love with him.

"I can't Polo."

Polo nodded his head, "It's still too soon huh? I know you loved Dre but I don't think he would object to you being happy again. I can make you very happy Nikki. That's all I want to do is make you happy."

I leaned back on the couch. "I know you would Polo but with everything going on it's not good timing."

Polo looked at me oddly. "When are you going to have Dre's funeral services? It's been almost a month since he passed."

That question took me off guard. I hadn't even thought about it. I still didn't want to let Polo know the FBI was protecting him.

"The coroner's office still has his body but I'm probably just gonna have a private service for him when they're done."

"Oh okay, let me know when." He looked at me sincerely. "Listen, I'm sorry. I shouldn't be rushing you into anything. I know you're still hurting and with this bitch ass nigga Malachi making you dance in his club I know this is stressful for you."

"Yeah," I sighed. "So, what are you going to do Polo? Are you still going to go after him?"

"No doubt. I got a plan in motion right now." He grinned then confidently spoke, "Pretty soon that nigga Malachi is going to be served up and I'll take over his shit."

"Well that's good to hear." I paused and then looked at him seriously. "Do you know who Malachi had shoot Dre? Was it Ricky or Reggie?"

Polo shrugged his shoulders. "I don't know who did it but both of them niggas are going to get the same thing Malachi is going to get so don't worry about it." He looked at his watch. "Nikki I gotta bounce. I have somebody I got to meet. I'll holla at you later." He got up and walked to the front door then turned around and looked at me. "You just be careful in that club and let me know if you hear anything I can use."

I nodded my head. "I will."

Polo opened the door and walked out to his. As I watched him pull off down the street I felt bad that I had to continue to lie to him about Dre's condition. He was going to be heartbroken when the truth came out but I couldn't risk him not following through with his plans to kill Malachi. As long as he was still alive none of us would be safe. An hour and half later I was out the door to pick Tyler up from daycare. I drove up in the parking lot, pulled into a parking space and turned off the engine. Just as I was about to get out of the car another car pulled up next to me.

"Nikki, I need you to come with me," a familiar voice

said.

I looked up and couldn't believe my eyes.

Jasmine

The hospital decided to discharge Kandi today and I went to South Fulton to pick her up. I went to her apartment to pick up some of her clothes. I also gathered some things to take to my condo before I headed to the hospital. It felt good doing this for her. I knew in my heart it was the right thing to do. There was no way I was going to let her go back to dancing at The Pink Palace. That life was not for her. I knew it the first night I saw her there but I didn't do the right thing and told her that. But that was then and this is now.

As I walked down the smelly hospital hallway I tried to hold my breath. I couldn't stand the smell of hospitals. Made me sick! I spotted Nurse Chauncey at the triage desk and he came out from around it to talk to me.

"So you're here to take Candice home?"

"Yeah, I'm glad she's doing better."

"She is. Her tests came back fine. Just make sure she stays away from all that extra activity at that club," he insisted.

I looked at him and smiled, "You don't have to worry about that. I'ma make sure she stays as far away from that club as possible." I put my hands on my hips, turned my head slightly to the side and looked at him. "By the way how do you know about that club?"

Chauncey gave me a sly grin. "Same way I knew you weren't really her sister. Besides I talked to her and she told me the story. She's lucky you and Nikki found her when y'all did. She could have easily died in that motel room."

"Oh, well, thank you for letting me be there for her."

He looked me up and down checking me out then focused on my eyes, "No problem. She needs all the friends she can get now and you look like a real good friend."

"I'm trying to be." I turned toward Kandi's room but Chauncey stopped me.

"Before you go can I ask you something?"

I turned back around. "Sure. What's on your mind?"

He stepped toward me. "Would you mind if I call you sometime? Maybe we could go out some where?"

I was taken back by his offer. I've never had a man dressed in scrubs ask me for my number before. I usually didn't date men unless I was on the clock but Nurse Chauncey was very different than the men I usual dealt with. Not to mention that he was fine as hell with his big brown eyes and handsome face.

"I think that would be nice," I replied. We took out our phones and exchanged numbers. Afterward, he went and got Kandi a wheelchair. I walked into her room and she was sitting up in bed.

"Hey Kandi, you ready to go?"

"Very ready," she eagerly replied. "I hate being in hospitals. The food sucks and it stinks."

We both exchanged laughter as I handed her the bag I packed from her apartment that contained clean clothes. Hurriedly she changed and a few minutes later she was dressed and ready to go. Chauncey came into the room pushing the wheelchair for Kandi.

"Here we go," Chauncey said and pushed the chair next to the bed for Kandi.

"Do I have to ride in that thing?" she pointed toward the wheelchair and began to protest. "My legs are fine. I can walk."

"Hospital policy," he replied.

"C'mon Kandi just get in so we can go. We have a lot of things to take care of," I told her. She sighed and then sat in the wheelchair. Chauncey smiled at me as we walked down to the hospital lobby. Once outside, Kandi jumped out of the chair and we laughed.

"You couldn't wait to do that huh?" Chauncey asked

between chuckles.

"You know it," she retorted.

"Well you take care of yourself Candice and I'll call you soon Jasmine."

I smiled at him. "I'm looking forward to it."

Kandi gave me a surprised look as we walked over to the parking garage to my car. "You two are going out?"

"Maybe. He asked me for my number so we'll see what happens."

"Well he is fine. But I thought you said you only mess with ballers with cash to spend. Chauncey is nice but he's a male nurse. Why the change of heart?" Kandi inquired.

"I don't know. Maybe I'm tired of the same old thing."

Chapter Seventeen

Daddy's Home

College Park, GA
Nikki

I couldn't believe my eyes when I saw Jayson Harper, Janelle's husband in the car next to me. I hadn't seen him in months. What was he doing at Tyler's daycare center?

"Jayson ... what are you doing here? Did something happen to Tyler?" I yelled as I jumped out of my car.

"No, no, calm down. Tyler is safe. He's at my house with Janelle but I need you to come with me now," he said seriously.

Jayson and I had a long history together. When I first met him five years ago I knew him by the alias

Tommy Holloway. He was running with a nigga named Damien who I was messing with, but in actuality he was an undercover police officer infiltrating the Flip Set drug organization. After I was raped and nearly beaten to death by Damien and his niggas, Jayson was the one who came to my rescue and took me to the hospital. I owed him my life so I trusted him completely. I quickly jumped in his car.

"What's going on Jayson? Why does Janelle have Tyler?" I asked him as he pulled out of the parking lot and turned onto the street. My heart was beating frantically as I awaited his answer.

"We just needed him to be somewhere safe."

I looked at him confused, then looked around as he drove. "Why? Where are we going Jay?"

He looked at me and smiled. "I'll explain everything once we get there. Trust me."

With his words, I nodded my head, took a deep breath and sat back. Less than ten minutes later, we were in a neighborhood in Morrow and we pulled up to a house and parked inside the garage.

I turned and looked at him. "Okay Jayson what's going on?"

"Come with me," he replied and got out of the car. I got out too and followed him into the house. By the smell, I could tell it was a new home, but it was empty. What the hell is going on, I thought and then I saw him standing in the living room. My mouth fell open, my heart started rapidly beating and I couldn't believe my eyes.

"Hey baby, I've missed you," Dre greeted. I looked at him like I had seen a ghost. My body began to tremble, and tears flooded my yes. I ran into his arms but unable to form words to speak. So many emotions flooded me at once. "It's okay Nikki. I'm here now."

Tears of joy streamed down my face. "Oh my God ... how ..."

"Come here baby have a seat." Dre led me to the couch.

He wiped the tears from my face and I looked at him again just to make sure my eyes weren't playing tricks on me or that this wasn't some kind of illusion.

"The FBI? The doctors told me the FBI took you into protective custody?"

"That would be me," Jayson spoke up. "I told the hospital to give everybody that story. We needed to get Dre somewhere safe."

"But why? I don't understand." I looked at Dre.

"Okay babe, let me explain." Dre took a deep breath then continued. "When I woke up in Emory I wanted to call you but realized that if Malachi knew I was out of my coma he would send somebody to kill me. I was already weak and couldn't protect you. I couldn't put you and Tyler in danger, so I needed to talk to someone I could trust and the first person I called was Jayson."

Jayson stepped closer. "After Dre got shot I started to investigate Malachi. I went back to The Pink Palace and started to watch his operation from the inside. Then one night I saw you walk up in there and you went straight to Malachi's office. I imagine you went there that night to make a deal with him to spare Dre's life?" he asked and I confirmed it with a head nod. "I couldn't let you know I was there so I decide to fall back and watch you. The next thing I knew you were back dancing at The Pink Palace and I could tell you weren't happy about it. A week later I got a call from Dre in the hospital and I filled him in on what was going on."

Dre nodded. "When Jayson told me that I knew that Malachi had eyes on you, so we knew I had to go somewhere safe to recover before we contacted you. I hated it but I knew it was the right thing to do. Jayson was the only other person I could trust."

"Did Janelle know about this too?" I asked Jayson.

He shook his head. "I just recently told her."

"No offense to you Jayson," I looked back at Dre, "but why do you keep on saying he was the only person you could trust? What about Polo? He's your best friend."

Dre frowned. "Who do you think shot me in the back?"

"What?" My chin dropped. "But Polo …"

"Is a snake ass nigga," Dre said with disgust. "The day in front of the shop when that white Crown Victoria screeched out in front of me, that punk ass nigga Reggie was behind the wheel and that bitch ass nigga Polo was sitting on the passenger side with a .45 in his hand pointing it at me."

Once again my chin hit the ground. "Oh my God … all this time he's been … Dre, I know why he did it."

"I do too," he confirmed with a scowl on his face. "So he could get rid of me, so he could get to you."

I grew even more disgusted with Polo than I was at Malachi. "That fucking traitor! I can't believe I felt sorry for him … I'm going to kill him!"

Dre caressed my face. "Not before I do."

I looked at Jayson, "I mean it Jayson. You can arrest me now cause he's a dead man."

Jayson nodded. "I understand how you feel. Believe me I do. What we're doing here now is completely off the books. I owed Dre this after what he did for Janelle," Jayson confirmed, referring to Dre killing my crazy ex-lover Damien. "But Malachi isn't going to rest until Dre is dead."

"Polo is going after him too," I informed them.

"How do you know? Last time we checked, Polo was trying to get down with his crew," Dre inquired.

"He's Don P. He's the one who sent those killers after Malachi in Lenox Mall."

"What? He's Don P?" Jayson said stunned and paced back and forth. "We've been trying to figure out for weeks who was behind that hit and everybody has been trying to find out who Don P is."

"He told me everything. He even wants me to give him information about when Malachi is most vulnerable so he can take him out," I told them.

"We can use this to our advantage," Jayson said to Dre looking at him.

"Yeah we can," he confirmed.

I stared at Dre. "Are you sure you're okay? You lost so much blood."

"I was in a lot of fucking pain and I've been popping painkillers like Tic Tac's. I was lucky the bullet didn't hit nothing vital. Once I got here and started rehab I started to gain my strength back. Jayson has been keeping me off of the police radar for the past month."

"I'ma give you guys some time to catch up," Jayson told us. "Janelle and I will keep Tyler at our place tonight."

Dre nodded, "Thanks man."

I got up and hugged Jayson, "Thank you for taking care of Dre."

"That's what family is for," he replied. "I'll be back

in the morning." Jayson left us alone. I still couldn't believe this was happening. I was with Dre and he was okay.

"I've missed you so much, Dre."

He stood up. "Not as much as I've missed you baby." Dre hugged me tight. "It's been torture knowing you were back at The Pink Palace dancing for that nigga."

"I'm so sorry baby," I said breaking down in tears. "I ... I ... had to ..."

"Ssshh. You don't have to tell me. I know you were trying to protect me, but I'm here now, and I'm going to protect you."

I kissed him with all the passion and love I had inside me. Dre pulled off my jacket and kissed my neck. My pussy instantly became moist, feeling his lips on my soft spot, and his big strong hands caressed my body. He pulled down the straps of my dress and it dropped to the floor. Dre stared at my half naked body, picked me up and carried me to the bedroom then laid me on the bed. We spent the next few hours making love like we never had before and for the first time in weeks I felt whole.

Jasmine

After we picked up more of Kandi's things from her apartment I settled her into a room in my condo. She was blown away by the size of my place and all of the amenities. We ordered a pizza and watched DVD's most of the night until she was tired and went to bed. She may not have wanted to admit it but she still needed more rest after her binge Sunday night.

The next day I took her grocery and clothing shopping for some new things. To be honest most of the clothes she had from her apartment weren't worth keeping. I wanted her to have a new look and a fresh start before she went back to Clark. Later on I planned on taking her down to the campus to get registered for fall classes. I was going to make sure she stayed on course this time around. As we were shopping at Old Navy in Buckhead Station my phone started to play Ludacris, "My Chick Bad" and I saw Chauncey's name illuminated on the display.

"Hello," I sang playfully.

"Hey Jasmine, how are you doing?"

I smiled like a school girl. "I'm doing good."

"How's Candice?"

"She's doing good. She's here with me and we're doing a little retail therapy."

"Sounds like fun." He paused then continued. "Listen, I was wondering if you'd like to go out for drinks tonight?"

I smirked. "Where?"

"The Apache Club. We can listen to a little jazz, drink a little something and get to know each other a little better."

"Sounds like fun."

"So can I pick you up?"

I hesitated for a moment. I never told dudes where I lived. "Ah, how about I picked you up instead?"

"Ah, sure. That's fine."

After Chauncey gave me his address, I hung up and finished shopping with Kandi. Later that night we stopped at Chipotle and got some food and headed home. It was time for me to get dressed and I was excited. It was weird because I hadn't been on a real date with a man in years. I had been so caught up in dancing and making money that I didn't even miss dating for fun. Besides I was fucking niggas who were giving me so much cash I didn't care if it wasn't a real date.

I decided to wear a black BCBG dress with a single twist strap over my left shoulder. It had a pleated waist with side knotted detail. I wore my hair down and put a little MAC makeup on my face. I walked out of my bedroom and saw Kandi on the couch flipping through television channels. She looked up at me and smiled.

"Damn, don't you look good! Poor Chauncey ain't going to know what to do with himself!"

"Well he better figure it out," I quipped and put on my wrap. "Don't wait up."

I walked out of the front door and to my car. Once inside I put Chauncey's address into my GPS and took off. Once I arrived at his house over on Lynn Avenue I parked in the driveway and walked up to his front door. I had butterflies in my stomach. This felt like a real first date. I rang his doorbell and a few seconds later Chauncey opened the door. He looked so damn handsome. This was my first time seeing him outside of his scrubs and he cleaned up well. He was wearing a white button down shirt with black jeans and black loafers. The scent of his Vera Wang cologne filled my nostrils and I was turned on.

"Wow … you look great," he droned, as he looked me up and down.

"You don't look half bad yourself Nurse Chauncey."

He grinned, "I'm off the clock. You can just call me Chauncey."

"Cool, are you ready to go?"

"Anywhere with you," he replied. We got in my car and I jumped on I-20 West toward midtown.

It had been a while since I had been to the Apache Club but after a couple of wrong turns we found the little club in the cut near the Varsity. We went inside and it was pretty much the same as I remembered. It was lowly lit with a live band playing in the front. It was a very eclectic club that had a gallery of erotic S&M pictures and paintings on the walls. Chauncey checked us in and we found a small table in the back. After the waitress took our drink orders Chauncey and I listened to the band on stage play a few sets. The waitress returned with my Long Island Iced Tea and his Hypnotic and grapefruit juice.

"They're good," I insisted to Chauncey.

"Yeah, they got a real original style. Kinda like you," he flirted.

"And what do you know about my style?"

"I've learned quite a bit about you." He took a sip of his drink.

I raised my eyebrow, "Like what?"

"Well I see you have quite a following on Facebook," he laughed.

"I guess I do. So are you a fan?"

"You didn't get my friend request?" he joked.

I laughed, "So what else do you know about me?"

Chauncey stared at me and then took another sip of his drink. "Well, it appears that you're an exotic dancer at The Pink Palace. You have calendars and posters for sale on your website. And you're a registered Democrat according to your Facebook page."

I sipped on my drink. "So did you know all this

before you asked me for my number?"

"No I didn't."

I started to feel weird sitting with him like he didn't know what type of chick I was. "So did you also go to The Pink Palace to watch me dance? Throw a couple of dollars on the stage?"

He shook his head and smiled. "I don't really do strip clubs."

I chuckled, "You don't? Why not?"

"Well, to me it's kind of like going to a restaurant and watching them cook a nice big juicy steak and not being able to eat it. If I wanna tease myself I'll just buy some porn," he joked, but I didn't laugh. "What's wrong?"

"I'm just wondering why you asked me out in the first place. I'm not exactly your type."

He raised his eyebrows. "And how do you know what's my type is?"

I sighed, "You're in the medical field. I'm sure you have dozens of nurses, doctors and interns you can ask out. You're not an ugly man."

"Thank you." He grinned. "That's true but why don't you think I would date somebody like you?"

I rolled my eyes, "You don't even know who I am."

"But that's the reason we're both here ... to get to know each other."

"Really? Sounds like you know everything already."

"Do you always try to sabotage the dates you go on?" he jested.

I took a swig of my iced tea, "Okay, you wanna get to know me? The real me?" I pursed my lips.

He put his hand underneath his chin and rested his elbows on the table. His eyes were affixed with mine and I had his full attention. "I'm dying to."

"Okay, let's put it all on the table. I'm a stripper."

"I already knew that," he quipped.

"I dance for money."

"Isn't that by definition what a stripper does?"

I arched my right eyebrow. "I normally don't fuck with guys like you. If you don't have money I don't have time for you."

He grinned. "But yet you're here with me so I'm doing something right."

"I'm bisexual."

He smiled. "Well that's great cause I like girls too."

I smirked. "I fuck for money if the price is right."

Chauncey sipped his drink. "After we have sex you'll pay me."

I looked at him and smirked. He caught me completely off guard because I wasn't expecting that little come back. I took another sip of my drink.

"Is that it? Is it my turn now?" he asked. I nodded my head for him to begin. "I'm a male nurse. I like my job. I was born and raised in North Philly by my grandparents. My mother died when I was six. Cancer. I never really knew my father … I saw him like three times a year or on holidays. He was bit of a crackhead. Clean one week a fiend the next. I moved to Atlanta last year and I rent my house. I hadn't met a woman that really interested me enough to date more than once or twice until this past Sunday night."

"Oh, thanks," I blushed, not knowing what else to say. I felt like an ass. He liked me despite of my lifestyle. "So you became a nurse because of your mother?" I asked, quickly changing the subject.

"Sorta. At first I wanted to become a doctor but I

really enjoyed talking to and helping patients more than just trying to fix them."

"That's great Chauncey. You're more than a nurse. You're definitely a people person."

"Exactly, and you're more than just a stripper. You're like a mini mogul. I imagine you make lots of money merchandising yourself like that. You got a real business mind mentality."

I smiled at him for acknowledging my business hustle. Most men only saw my tits and ass and thought I had nothing else going for me in life.

"Well I did graduate from Spelman so I might as well put all that hard work to use."

He held up his glass in a toast. "Smart and sexy. You're a rare breed Jasmine."

"You're pretty remarkable yourself Chauncey." I raised my glass and we toasted.

The waitress returned and we ordered another round of drinks and continued to get to know each other. We started to talk about everything from politics to music and I found myself digging this man's mind just as much as I did his body. Chauncey was a great guy, not to mention sexy as hell, and the more we talked and drank I found myself getting hornier by the second.

The next thing we knew it was two o'clock in the morning and we decided to head out. I drove Chauncey back to his house and pulled up in his driveway.

"Well maybe next time I can pick you up," he joked.

"Yeah, maybe next time you will," I confirmed.

Chauncey smiled then leaned over and kissed me softly. My pussy started to dance. He pulled away and opened his car door.

"I know this is usually the other way around, but you know ... since you picked me up for this date and you're taking me home," Chauncey rambled, "anyway, do you wanna come in for a night cap?"

I stared at his fine ass for a second and pictured him with no clothes on. "Yeah, I'd love a night cap."

We got out of the car and walked to his front door. Chauncey fumbled with his keys until he found the right one and opened it. He flipped on the lights and turned around and took my wrap from me and hung it on his coat hanger. He turned and looked at me. Before I knew it, I grabbed him by his shirt and pulled him closer to me. We kissed, allowing our tongues to dance.

"What about the night cap?" he asked, pulling away from me.

"Fuck it. I'll drink it in the morning." I kissed him again.

Chauncey took me to his bedroom and we awkwardly moved around his room until we reached his bed. He pulled my twisted strap down over my left shoulder and my dress hit the floor. I stood in my Victoria's Secret black lace bra and panties and then Chauncey turned me around and unfastened my bra, letting it join my dress on the floor. His hands cupped my soft titties as he kissed my neck. My pussy was dripping with excitement.

I turned around and unzipped his jeans as he unbuttoned his shirt. I wanted him so bad. More than any man I had been with in a long time. My hands found his manhood and it felt like he was swinging a baseball bat between his thighs. I sat on the bed behind me and pulled his jeans and boxers down and his long thick dick popped up in front of my face. I licked his swollen mushroom tipped head like a lollipop before I took him to the back of my throat. Chauncey threw his head back as I had my way with him, sucking the skin off his juicy stick. He placed one hand under my chin and the other behind my head and moved his member in and out of my mouth letting my saliva provide moisture. He tasted so good.

He soon pulled out before he released his seeds in my mouth then pushed me back on his bed. He licked my neck then traced his tongue down my chest to my rock hard nipples. He sucked the left, then the right, then continued his journey down south. He dropped to his knees as his tongue licked my belly. Chauncey licked down my inner thighs making my pussy jealous. It was trickling with cream and soon he tasted my flavor. He pushed my legs apart giving himself plenty of room to enjoy his meal. If I didn't know better I would have sworn that Chauncey was an OB/GYN instead of a nurse cause he knew my pussy like he had been there before. The sound of my moans echoed in his room as I rode the waves of my coming orgasm.

Chauncey stood up, went into the nightstand next to his bed and pulled out a condom. He ripped it opened, stroked his hardness, then rolled the condom on. He climbed on top and kissed me. I wasn't used to so much kissing but with him, I liked it. He pushed his dick into my creamy tunnel and I clamped down on his thickness. Most men just started pumping and fucking the shit outta me at this point but Chauncey took his time and grinded pussy making me cream even more. I wrapped my legs behind his back keeping him deep in me. He sucked my neck; I scratched his back, and sang his name like I was recording a demo. Most of the time I faked shit just to stroke a nigga's ego, but the way Chauncey was stroking my pussy it drove me crazy. He pulled out of my wetness and I begged for him to put it back. Begging was totally unheard of for me but there I was begging for his dick. Chauncey grinned and turned me over flat on my stomach. Once I was positioned the way he wanted, he spread my legs apart and re-entered my pussy from the back. This time he groaned like a beast. He was lying on my back and gave me the business. I demanded that he fuck me as I pushed my ass back at him. His stomach clapped against my ass giving us the applause we deserved for our performance. There was no rest for us tonight.

👑 👑 👑 👑 👑 👑 👑 👑 👑 👑 👑 👑 👑 👑 👑 👑

The morning came and I was wrapped in Chauncey's arms, exhausted and exulted, from our lovemaking. My hair was a mess. His bed was soaked. I stared at him and smiled, "Okay you were right. How much do I owe you?"

He smiled, "Don't worry I'ma start a tab."

"Cool. My credit is good."

"But your sex is better," Chauncey added.

I snuggled my head in his chest, "And you're incredible."

"You seduced me."

"You invited me in. I think I'll take that night cap now."

"I got you," he laughed and caressed my ass. It felt so good.

I didn't wanna fool myself into thinking this was going to be any more than what it was so I didn't say any more. All this time I never thought I would meet a man who could make me feel as good as a woman did, but being with Chauncey proved I didn't know what the hell I was talking about.

Chapter Eighteen

My Word is Law

Atlanta, GA
Malachi

I finally worked out the details of my deal with Carlos my new connect out of Miami. This was vital for me to keep my grip on the streets. Ricky was picking up my first shipment today. I was still on guard and looking to find this Don P before he tried to kill me again. Not knowing who this pussyhole made me paranoid. I couldn't trust anybody. I never did before but now I couldn't put anything past nobody. I sent Latoya and Courtney to New Orleans to stay with her parents. I didn't need them to be in the line of fire again.

Now was the perfect time to bring sweet Nikki into

my world completely. It was time to put her in her place and make her my woman. I needed to taste that sweet pussy again. No need to pretend like she had a choice in the matter any longer.

My phone rang. "What is it?" I spat.

"Jasmine wants to come up and see you boss," Bump replied.

She probably wanted some cash for ass. That was okay. My dick needed to feel some tight pussy. "Send her up."

"Okay," Bump replied and hung up.

A few seconds later he brought her up to my office and she was dressed in jeans and a tee shirt. Not ready to work but maybe just here to fuck. I loved the way this bitch worked, always on her hustle.

I grinned at her. "Hello sweet Jasmine you needed to see me?"

She smiled and sat in the chair in front of my desk. "As a matter of fact I do."

I leaned back in my chair. "Business or pleasure?"

"Everything is business, Malachi. But I need to talk to you about one of the little niggas in your crew."

"Another one of them niggas getting rude wit the girls?"

"Worse," she exhaled. "The other night at Reggie's party that nigga Chaz and two others took a girl named Kandi up out of here. She was high and fucked up. They took her to a motel and she nearly OD'd. They just left her there to die," Jasmine explained.

My eyebrows crinkled, "Is da bitch dead?"

She frowned, "No she's not. But if Nikki and I hadn't got to her in time she would be."

"Nikki and you?" I asked with a raised eyebrow.

"You two are spending time together now?"

"Not really, but she was the one who called me and told me what was happening."

"I heard Nikki put on a good show for Reggie." I smiled at Jasmine. "You like her?"

She rolled her eyes and leaned forward in her chair. "Malachi, what does that have to do with anything? Didn't you hear what I said? Chaz left Kandi to die in a sleazy motel room," she said upset.

I shrugged my shoulders, "What do you want me to do about it?"

Jasmine threw her hands up, "Fuck that nigga up!"

"For what? If these bitches want to get high and kill themselves I can't stop dat. As long as her ass doesn't die in my club, I don't give a damn."

Jasmine stood up, "Really? So that's it? You don't give a fuck?"

I didn't respond cause I didn't care.

"All you care about up in here is Nikki?" She paused then chuckled, "Then I suggest you check your stupid little brother."

I glared at her, "What does dat mean?"

She walked to the door then turned around, "It means that he tried to take some pussy from your number one bitch in the locker room Sunday night. Guess he's trying to be like you. Still don't give a damn huh?" Jasmine walked out. I turned around in my chair, looking down at the club from my window and saw Reggie sitting at a booth getting a lap dance. My blood boiled looking at him. I told that asshole to stay away from her and he pulled this?

I got up and marched downstairs with Bump following closely behind me. I walked up to Reggie in the booth with the bitch in his lap.

"Get da fuck up," I yelled to the bitch and she jumped up.

"Dang bruh, I was just getting a little bull ride," he said happily. Instantly, I slapped the shit out of him. Reggie fell back in the booth. "Mala! What you do that for!"

I punched his bumbaclot ass as he tried to cover himself. Reggie fell on the floor and I kicked him. Anger was in my eyes. He always fucked up! I grabbed a beer bottle from the table and busted it over his head and blood ran down his face. "Malachi please! No more!"

"I told yuh not to touch her. But ya still tess me! If yuh weren't my brother I would kill yuh bumbaclot ass now." I glared at him, "Go clean yourself up."

Everybody in the club stared at me with fear. I stared back at them and they all went back to their business. I had to set an example to them all. Not even my brother could tess me and not suffer. Now I had to go check on Nikki and made sure she knew that my word was law.

Nikki

Waking up in Dre's arms was the best feeling in the world. We spent the night making love until we couldn't move. A few hours later Jayson called and said he was on his way back over with Janelle and Tyler.

The garage door opened and Jayson parked inside then we heard the side door open and in walked Janelle carrying Tyler in her arms. His little eyes lit up when he saw his daddy standing in front of him and he reached his little arms toward him.

"Daddy!"

"Hey there big man! You miss Daddy?" Dre asked. Tyler answered with a tight and head nod. I had never seen Tyler so happy. He was his father's son for real. Dre exhaled and held on to his son. I hugged them both and for the first time in months our family was whole. After Dre spent a few hours playing with Tyler I put him down for a nap in the bedroom and all four of us sat in the living room and tried and figure out our next move.

"I didn't realize how much I missed him," Dre said happily.

"He's missed you too," Janelle added.

Jayson got up, walked to the window and peeped outside.

"Who's place is this Jayson?" I asked him.

"It's a safe house we use to protect witnesses before a trial. It was currently not being used and was perfect for us," he enlightened. "I've dug into the club business records down at city hall and the previous owner of The Pink Palace was named Leroy Love Jr., who's body was found in a landfill in Decatur last year. There are no records of Malachi having ownership of the club on file and we have no evidence linking Malachi to Leroy's murder … but we can all assume what happened."

"Malachi killed him and took over his club," I said.

Jayson nodded. "And now, you said Polo is gunning for Malachi?"

"Yes. He's going by the name Don P."

"Hmm," Jayson turned and looked at Dre. "As much as you hate Polo we may be able to use him to take care of Malachi. I know you wanna kill him but murdering him in cold blood on the streets is going to bring police attention to you and I can't protect you from that."

Dre leaned back on the couch, "I know that. I've been thinking the same thing too. If we can get them to go after each other that would be perfect. Either Polo will kill Malachi or he'd kill Polo. Or they'd kill each other."

"But how do you get them to do that?" Janelle asked.

"We tell Malachi who Polo is," I told her.

"Not you," Dre said firmly. "You're not setting a foot back in that club."

"Besides Malachi would be suspicious of that information coming from you," Jayson added.

I thought about it for a moment then smiled, "I may have a way of letting him find out from a source he would trust."

Dre looked at me oddly, "Who?"

"Jasmine. She works in the club and she's Malachi's number one money maker. She's real close to him."

"But can you trust her?" Dre asked.

"We've gotten close and I think if I can show her the benefit to her in doing this for me, she will."

Jayson folded his arms, "I don't know. It sounds too risky. I've seen Jasmine at the club and she's the type that only makes moves if it makes money for her. I think if we can tie Malachi to the shoot out at Lenox that might be a better way to take him down."

"But it doesn't solve our problem with Polo," I pointed out. "Trust me Jayson, I know what type of woman Jasmine is. I used to be just like her. I know how to get through to her. We've gotten close recently."

"Are you sure you can trust her?" Dre asked again.

"I'm sure." I looked in his eyes. "This is the best way we can solve all of our problems without directly putting ourselves at risk."

"Okay I trust you," Dre confirmed.

"If you say you can do it then I believe you," Janelle added.

Jayson was still thinking it over. He, more than anyone of us, knew the danger involved in playing both sides of the fence. He was deep cover for eight months infiltrating the Flip Set clique. Somebody also betrayed him whom he thought he could trust and took a bullet because of it. So he knew what was at stake.

"Okay ... we'll do it, but no direct contact with Malachi. I will be following you when you make contact with Jasmine". Jayson insisted.

"That's fine." I agreed.

"Okay, so let's figure out where and when this will all go down," Jayson announced.

For the next few hours we all discussed and planned how we would take both of these fools down. Once we decided on a course of action Janelle and Jayson decide to give Dre, Tyler, and me some more time alone. It felt like it had been years since we had all been together as a family. I felt like my family and life were forever ruined because of the mess and I realized I would do anything to protect the ones I loved.

Dre looked at me sitting on the couch, "So are you still going to marry me?"

I could feel my heart swelling with happiness hearing him ask me that. "There's nothing more I want to do. I still have the ring at home. I had to take it off because ..."

"I know. We've been through so much bullshit over the years." He shook his head. "You did what you had to do for us Nikki, so I'm going to also do the same. I love you."

I leaned over and kissed him, "I love you too." I leaned back and pulled out my phone. "I guess it's time to set things up." I began to dial Jasmine's number. After the second ring she answered.

"Hey Nikki? Wus up?"

"Hey Jasmine, I need to talk to you about something very important."

"Okay, cool. What's up?"

I looked at Dre and winked. "Can we meet somewhere and talk?"

"Sure, where?"

"How about Borders in midtown on Ponce De Leon in about an hour?" I suggested.

"Sounds good. I'll see you then."

We both ended our calls and I looked at Dre. "Everything is all set up. I'll call Jayson and tell him to be there and blend in with the shoppers."

"Okay, babe. I trust you."

As if on cue, my phone started to ring and I saw Malachi's name on the display.

I glanced up at Dre. "It's Malachi."

Dre scowled, "This nigga got nerve. Answer it."

"What the hell do you want?" I asked, taking his call.

"My dear Nikki, I've been missing you."

I sucked my teeth, "I don't give a damn."

"I've warned you about your mouth. You need to learn to listen or I'll have to teach you to," he said callously.

"And you need to learn when to fuck off! I'm done dancing for you. You and that club can kiss my ass!"

"You're trying my patience Nikki. Get your ass to

this club now or there will be consequences for your actions. Once I start things, I don't stop. You will learn," Malachi warned me menacingly.

I rolled my eyes, "Save your threats for someone who gives a damn. You come after me and I got something for that ass nigga! So go eat a dick and stay the hell away from me," I yelled and hung up on his ass.

Dre smiled and clapped his hands. "I couldn't have said that better myself."

Chapter Nineteen

A Common Enemy

Midtown Atlanta, GA
Jasmine

After my chat with Malachi, I lost all respect for that nigga. I had always had a certain level of respect for him more than anybody else at the club. After all he was the head nigga in charge. I understood that he was a gangster and not a gentleman. Especially when it came to our business transactions. He paid me top dollar to dance at The Pink Palace and for sex. We never pretended it was anything other than that.

The bullshit he said about not giving a damn about any bitch in his club really pissed me off. At that moment he became another trick in my eyes and I was done fucking with him. I could dance at Magic City, Strokers, or The Pink Pony South and make just as much money if not more. I was glad I told him what his nasty little brother tried to do to Nikki. He needed his ass kicked. I was surprised to get a call from Nikki asking me to meet her at Borders. I knew whatever it was she wanted to discuss was important. I had been dying for weeks to know what was going on between her and Malachi and I just may find out.

I walked into Borders and saw folks browsing around. I even spotted the new Eric Jerome Dickey novel in his Gideon series that I wanted to read. I would have to remind myself to pick it up on the way out. I then spotted Nikki sitting by herself at a table in the Seattle Coffee section, sipping on a coffee, waiting for me. I walked over to her.

"I hope you weren't waiting long," I told her and sat down.

"Naw, I just got here a few minutes ago myself. I love the coffee here. By the way how's Kandi?"

"She's actually doing much better. I moved her in with me a few days ago."

Nikki's eyebrows raised, "Really? I guess you were serious about trying to be a friend to her."

"Yeah, she needs good people around her now. I'm not exactly sure if I'm that person but I'm all she's got. Her days of dancing at The Pink Palace are done. I'm going to make sure she goes back to Clark and finish her education."

"I have a feeling Kandi is in good hands," Nikki confirmed.

"So what's up?" I asked, looking at her. "Why do you need to speak to me?"

Nikki took another sip of her coffee then put it on the table. "Well, I have a serious problem with Malachi and I need your help to solve it."

I crossed my legs under the table and leaned back in my chair. "I know there's something going on between you two but you've never wanted to talk about it before. So why now?"

"Things have changed for me. I've found a way from up under his thumb permanently," Nikki said seriously.

"Okay, I need you to explain it to me. Everything."

Nikki sighed. She looked at the table and then back at me, "Alright. If I'm going to ask you for your help I might as well tell you the truth." She paused momentary and gathered her thoughts. "My fiancé Dre, who is also the father of my child, used to do business with Malachi a few years ago. This was before Malachi owned The Pink Palace."

"You mean when you used to dance there?"

"Correct. Dre was getting his supply from Malachi, but when he got arrested the police took his supply and he took a big loss. Fortunately Dre had some great lawyers on his case and he was able to beat a lot of the charges he was facing and only did a year in prison. When he got out he was done with the drug game and I was done with my life at The Pink Palace. Unfortunately Dre still owed Malachi a lot of money but he was able to make a deal to pay him back his money over a period of time."

"Let me guess, once Dre paid him back what he owed him Malachi still wanted more."

"Yeah, he wanted more. But Dre wasn't going to pay him. So Malachi had Dre shot right in front of my baby and me," Nikki said regrettably. I could see the sadness on her face recalling that memory.

"Damn. I'm sorry Nikki."

"It's okay. Dre didn't die. He fell into a coma and by this time I was desperate to do anything to stop Malachi from finishing the job he already started. So I went to him and made a deal."

"That was the night I saw you walk up in the club and headed straight for his office. I was wondering who the hell you were and why Malachi let you in," I said and chuckled to myself.

"Yeah ... that night." Nikki shook her head. "That dirty muthafucka said that if I danced in The Pink Palace I could work off the debt Dre owed him. But I knew this sick bastard just wanted me up in there for his enjoyment."

"That explains so much, like why you never wanted to be there." Nikki nodded her head. "So what's changed now?"

Nikki sighed, "Dre's awake now. He's been awake for weeks and getting better. I've been lying to Malachi saying that he's dead." She had an anxious expression on her face.

"Shit ... that's a dangerous game you're playing Nikki. So why don't you all just get the fuck outta town?"

"Cause there's another problem."

"Like?"

"The nigga who shot Dre was also his best friend Polo."

My mind searched my memory bank. Then my eyebrows raised when I realized who he was. "Polo, that nigga that's always with Reggie? That's Dre's best friend? Why would he stab his boy in the back like that?"

"Because of me. Polo said that he's been in love with me for years. I guess he saw his chance to get rid of Dre and get at me."

"Well aren't you just little Miss Poplar?" I joked. "Does Polo know Dre's alive?"

"No. He's held up somewhere safe right now."

"This is one hell of a shit hole you got yourself into Nikki but I don't see how I can help you."

Nikki leaned in closer to the table. "Would you help me?"

"If I could? Yeah."

"Why?"

"Because I can't stand Malachi's ass," I said frankly.

"Wow, I kinda thought you two had something going on?"

I rolled my eyes, "That was strictly business and I'm done fucking with his ass on that tip. After what happened to Kandi, and him telling me he didn't give a shit, that just told me it's time to move the fuck on."

"I could've told you that a long time ago," she said and laughed.

"Yeah ... so why do you feel like you can trust me all of a sudden?"

Nikki looked into my eyes, "I don't know. Maybe because I feel like in some ways when I look at you I see a lot of myself. I think you see that too," she said with a raised eyebrow.

I shook my head and chuckled. "I hate to admit it ... but I do too. I see you and I wonder what my future is going to be. It's just weird."

"Jasmine, your future is whatever you want it to be. Besides, where you are with your game, I never was.

You have a business mind like I've never seen in a bitch," Nikki joked.

"Why thank you," I replied with a smile. "But getting back to my question, what makes you think I can help you?"

"Well, you know the beef that Malachi is having with this Don P nigga?"

"Yeah, Malachi is so uptight about it he ain't going nowhere unless he's thirty deep."

Nikki picked up her coffee and sipped it, "What if I told you I know who that nigga Don P is? How much money do you think Malachi will pay for that information?"

I uncrossed my legs and leaned forward on the table. "A nice penny or two. You're saying you know who he is?"

"Yep."

"But how does that help you with your situation?"

She narrowed her eyes, "Because that foul ass nigga Polo is Don P."

I was shocked. "What?"

"Yep." She nodded her head. "So we have a plan to set them fools up. We just need somebody who Malachi would trust to deliver that info."

I grinned, "Oh I get it. So they can take each other out for you. That is brilliant."

"And it can also be profitable for you." Nikki rubbed her fingers together. "Malachi would pay top dollar to find this shit out."

"Yes he would ... but you know what?

Her eyebrows arched. "What?"

"I would do it for free if it meant getting rid of Malachi," I said with a big ol' smile on my face.

Nikki laughed and took my hand, "But the cash is just an extra motivator!"

"Exactly," I confirmed and laughed with her. "So what do you need me to do?"

After Nikki explained the plan she and Dre came up with to eliminate both Malachi and Polo we parted ways. As I headed home, I thought about how dangerous of a game this was that I was about to play but to get Malachi out of my life, it was also worth it. I still couldn't believe the story Nikki told me about what that foul ass nigga had done to her. And I was even more shocked about Polo. I had always seen him around Reggie hanging out at The Pink Palace looking shifty. He always gave me a bad vibe and now I knew why. That snake shot his own best friend to get at his woman. How foul can someone get?

The plan that Nikki came up with was airtight and it was going down Saturday night. I just needed to get Malachi to believe my story and I would get paid in the meantime. Maybe a cool $25-30g's he would pay for what I knew. Even if things went bad and Malachi survived the set up I would still be in the clear with the money. I just hoped he caught a hot one between his eyes for all the pain he had caused Nikki and her family.

I was also excited about tonight as well. Chauncey was coming over to my place for dinner. It was the first time I had ever brought a man back to my condo. I didn't know what it was but there was something about him I found simply irresistible, not to mention arousing. This was the first time in a long time I had found myself so drawn to a man. He excited me, not only physically, but mentally too. I couldn't believe out of all the niggas I had fucked with—players, athletes, and gangsters—that I was dating a male nurse of all people. This was crazy for me. I soon reached home and looked at my watch. It was 5:30 pm and Chauncey said he'd be over at 8 pm so that gave me just under three hours to cook and get ready for dinner. I went inside and a delicious smell greeted me.

"Hey Jasmine! You're running behind schedule for your date," she noted, standing over the stove stirring something inside of a pot.

"I know," I blushed but was relieved. "Thanks for starting dinner for me."

Kandi giggled, "No problemo! Besides, I'm glad you hit it off with Nurse Chauncey," she winked.

I walked into the kitchen and opened the oven and saw the beef flank cooking very well. "Don't call him that when he gets here. When he's off work, he's just Chauncey."

"Okay, that's cool. I just can't believe you two are on a second date. He must have really put it on you the other night," Kandi commented and put her finger seductively in her mouth.

I couldn't help but smile at her sexy ass wearing a floral sundress. If I wasn't feeling Chauncey so much I might've had to seduce her again. "Yes he did and he's gonna put it on me again tonight!"

"Ooohhh, mind if I watch?" Kandi inquired playfully.

"You know me, I don't give a damn. Cause I know you gonna hear some moaning and groaning tonight," I insisted.

Kandi laughed hard and so did I cause we both know I wasn't lying. I headed to my room and picked out my clothes for dinner. Going through my tons of clothes, I decided upon a blue Michael Kors wrap mini dress and matching Chanel shoes.

I wanted to feel sexy so I went and ran the water in my tube for a Tokyo Milk bubble bath. After an hour of soaking my body in the soothing bath solution I got up and got dressed. I decided to wear my hair up to show off my neck. Chauncey loved sucking on it so I wanted to tease him all night. By the time I got done fixing my hair and applying my makeup I heard my doorbell chime and looked at my alarm clock and saw that it was 8 o'clock on the dot. Chauncey was prompt.

I heard Kandi open the door for him and he was happy to see her. I stepped out of my room looking fierce and once again his eyes lit up when he saw me.

"Wow, I feel under dressed now," Chauncey said referring to his red Karl Kani shirt and matching black jeans.

"Not at all. I just wanted to look good for you tonight," I told him.

"I don't think you couldn't," Chauncey droned and walked over to me.

Kandi winked at me and licked her lips behind his back letting me know Chauncey looked good enough to eat. I winked back acknowledging her.

"Are you hungry?"

Chauncey grinned, and looked me up down "Very."

"For food," I smirked.

"Yeah, whatever that is you got in there smells good."

"Why thank you," Kandi said. I cut my eyes at her.

"What?" he laughed at the expression on my face. I wanted him to think I cooked it. "So you didn't cook, huh?"

"Well, I was running late and Kandi was nice enough to start it for me."

"And finish it," he added.

I rolled my eyes, "Details." I led him to the living room and he had a seat on the couch.

"This is a real nice place you got here Jasmine. Like something outta MTV Cribs," he joked.

I looked around my place and shrugged. "It's cozy."

"Well, I'll put dinner on the table for you and give you two some privacy," Kandi told us.

"Thank you," I said and she disappeared into the kitchen.

"I'm glad to see she's doing better. I knew you would take good care of her," Chauncey affirmed.

"I'm trying." I sat down next to him. "I'm glad you came over. I don't normally invite men over here."

"Then I feel special to be the first."

"You should," I joked and Chauncey leaned over and kissed me. Damn, I could feel myself getting wet. What was this man doing to me?

We heard Kandi clear her throat, "Dinner is on the table y'all."

"Thank you Kandi," we said in unison.

"I'll be in my room," she crooned and bounced away.

We both moved to the dining room and took a seat. I was amazed at how everything looked and smelled. Kandi did her thing. Beef flank, roasted potatoes, and collard greens sat on the table in front of us. If I knew she could cook like this I would have moved her in a long time ago. Chauncey picked up a bottle of Moscato that was chilling and the corkscrew. He opened it and poured us both a glass.

"Can I make a toast?" he asked.

"Sure."

"To getting to know each other even better," he said. We drank to that. We both dug into our food and it was delicious. Kandi should have been a chef instead of a stripper. After dinner we retreated to the living room and I turned on the stereo. R. Kelly featuring Keri Hilson's "Number One" started to play in the background. We sat on the couch together.

Chauncey looked in my eyes. "Let me ask you something Jasmine, where do you see yourself in five years?"

I thought about it. "I want to own a business, something in the entertainment field. I haven't really mapped it out yet."

"Maybe you should start," he replied.

"I got a question for you."

He smiled, "Shoot."

"Why are you still dating me after I told you what my lifestyle was like?"

He caressed my arm. "I like you. A lot."

"Seriously. I'm not the type of girl you bring home to momma."

"My momma is dead, remember?" he smirked.

"Sorry," I shook my head embarrassed as hell. "I shouldn't have said that."

"Relax. Listen, I don't like to judge people until I get to know them. And from what I've learned from being around you is that you're a funny, sexy, smart and caring woman. All the things I like in a woman, Jasmine." He touched my face.

"Jacqueline. My real name is Jacqueline."

I didn't know why I told him that. It just felt right.

"Jacqueline? I like that." He leaned over and kissed my lips and my heart fluttered. I couldn't believe it. I could actually be falling for this guy. How the hell did that happen? One day I was 'Money Over Niggas' the next thing I know I was dating a nurse? Whatever, this felt right and so did the way he touched my leg. His hand traveled further up my thick chocolate thigh until he was under my dress and he touched my fire.

He pulled away, "You're not wearing any panties."

"Hmmm, I must have forgotten to put them on," I said and smiled.

Chauncey kissed me again and put his thumb on my swollen clit and rubbed me the right way. "Aahh," I moaned and it felt like a river flowing between my thighs. Chauncey inserted his index finger into my tight hole and I began to grind. My hand caressed his dick in his jeans and he was harder than a brick. I unzipped his fly and pulled out his beautiful, long, thick dick. I gripped it and rubbed it up and down. He groaned as I stroked his manhood. I couldn't take it anymore and decided to straddle him right there on the couch. Chauncey let out a lustful hiss as I slid down his meaty shaft. My dress was bunched up around my waist exposing my fat ass as I ponied up and down on his dick driving him crazy. R. Kelly's "Echo" provided the sound track to our lust. As we were getting our freak on I spied Kandi poking her head out of her room down the hall with a shit-eating grin on her face watching us. Chauncey's head was tilted back with his eyes closed unaware of our audience. I mouthed the words "Go away" and she stuck her tongue out and mouthed back "No" and covered her mouth, giggling. I shook my head, and refocused my attention on Chauncey. He pulled off his shirt and then lifted my dress up over my head leaving me only in my Chanel shoes. He wrapped his arm around my waist and stood up while his dick was still deep in me.

"Where's your bedroom?" he grunted lustfully.

"That way," I pointed down the hall. Kandi quickly darted back in her room before she was spotted by Chauncey. He carried me down the hallway while I was still riding his dick like a jockey. He pushed the door open and walked in and I made sure I grabbed the door and slammed it shut. Kandi's little nasty self wasn't going to watch the rest of our private show.

Chapter Twenty

Judas Kiss

College Park, GA
Nikki

After my talk with Jasmine I was happy she was onboard and ready to help us take down Malachi. Jayson was sitting a few tables away from us pretending to read a book and he heard most of what was said. When Jasmine left, Jayson came over to my table, and I confirmed everything that we talked about.

Now it was time for phase two of our plan. I had to give Polo the story we cooked up and make him believe it. Dre hated this part and didn't want me anywhere near him. I didn't want to be in the same room with that bitch ass nigga but this had to done and I was the only one who could do it. After finally convincing Dre that I would be safe around Polo, Jayson agreed to be nearby if anything went left. I left Borders, went back to my house and called Polo, inviting him over. A few minutes later he was ringing my doorbell.

I took a deep breath and walked to the door, "Hey Polo."

"Wus up Nikki," Polo replied and came inside. I closed the door behind him and we went to the living room and took a seat on the couch. "So you said on the phone you had something important to tell me about Malachi?" he asked with a concerned expression on his face.

"Yeah, you told me I should tell you if I overheard something important."

He nodded, "Yeah, what is it?

I looked him in the eyes and I saw the eagerness. Snake ass nigga, I thought. "Well, I was with Malachi last night."

Polo frowned, "You were with him?"

"No, not like that. I was in his office when he got a phone call."

"Oh. Okay." He exhaled.

"I really couldn't hear what the other person on the other end was saying but Malachi was stressing that he needed the shipment in on Saturday night. He said he was going to be there himself to make sure nothing went wrong."

"Shipment?" Polo repeated. "He found a new supplier?"

I nodded, "That's my assumption."

"Did he say where this drop was going down at?"

"He said something about a warehouse in Hapeville

… four o'clock in the morning." I paused as if I were trying to recall more information. "He said something about Airport Loop Road … Forrest Avenue and um … the old storage warehouse?" I shook my head for more effect. "I wish I knew more details."

Polo smiled, "Don't worry about it Nikki, you've given me all the information I need. I promise you I'm gonna kill that nigga for what he did to Dre."

The hairs on the back of my neck rose when I heard him say that. For what he did to Dre? You dirty ass mutherfucka! You shot Dre! You betrayed your best friend! You want to take me away from the father of my child, you bitch ass nigga, I screamed in my head. It took all of myself control to not take my razorblade out of my pocket and cut his throat. I held onto my rage and I smiled.

"Thank you Polo. I don't know what I would do if you weren't here for me."

He took my hand, "Like I told you Nikki, I'm always going to be there for you. And I hope soon you let me take care of you for real."

I threw up a little in my mouth. "You don't know what it means to hear you say that to me Polo."

He leaned in to kiss me and I wanted to turn my head but I let him do it. He made me sick and I pulled away from him.

Polo exhaled deeply. I guess he was annoyed that I wasn't throwing myself at him. "I know it's too soon for you but I can't help myself."

"I promise you Polo, once you take care of Malachi you'll get everything you ever wanted plus more," I said seductively and he smiled. "But, in the meantime, I'm really tired, I need to get some rest."

I got up off the couch and walked to the door. Polo followed behind me and then he did the unthinkable. He grabbed my ass. I wanted to slap the shit outta him. "I hope this is part of the plus more," he leaned in and whispered in my ear.

I turned around and faced him, "You will find out very soon."

Polo grinned and I wanted to kill him right there. I opened the door and he walked out. I quickly closed and locked it behind him. "The only thing you're going to get is the same thing you gave Dre ... a bullet in your ass!" I said out loud.

Jasmine

After the workout Chauncey gave me last night I was surprised I could walk straight. My pussy was sore that much was for sure but it felt so good. I couldn't believe how fast I was falling for this man. Hell, any man. I love women and I thought if I had any kind of relationship in the future it would be with one. But along came Nurse Good Dick and I was begging for that thing like a fiend.

Chauncey left an hour ago and I dragged myself out of bed and into the shower. I pulled on my robe and walked out to the kitchen and saw Kandi cooking breakfast. She gave me a mischievous grin.

"I heard someone sing a new song last night, Ooohhh Chauncey, do to me like that baby! You blowing my back, baby, Your dick's at my g-spot, you making my bedrock," Kandi sang remixing the lyrics from "Bedrock."

"Shut up," I smiled. "I was not that loud."

"Whatever."

"You must've had your ear to my door," I accused her and had a seat at the table. "I can't believe you were watching us fuck last night."

"How was I supposed to know you would be getting busy on the couch?" Kandi handed me a plate of scrambled eggs and bacon. "So you really like him huh?"

I smiled and took a fork full of eggs, "Maybe."

"Bullshit! Nurse Chauncey got you open and you know it."

"Whatever, I enjoy his company. We click together."

She gave me a sly smile and sat with me at the table. "I know. I saw you two clicking hard last night."

"Shut up," I laughed but then I became serious. "I don't know. It's more than just a physical thing." I put my fork down, "He understands me. He doesn't judge me. I've never met a man like him before."

"I can feel the love in the air," Kandi crooned.

I couldn't even argue with her on that one. I wasn't going to force anything to happen. I was just going to wait and see what happened between us. Thoughts of what Nikki told me yesterday still played in my head. Tonight was the night to set things into motion. It was a risky move but I really want to get rid of Malachi. I frowned just thinking about him. He had been doing too much dirt to everybody not to get his in return. "Kandi I want you to know you can stay here as long as you want rent free. Just as long as you get back in school and make something of yourself. I don't want you ever setting foot in a strip club to work again."

Kandi looked at me stunned, "I will Jasmine. I can never thank you enough for everything you've done for me."

"Just you succeeding in life is thanks enough."

Kandi got up and hugged me.

♛ ♛ ♛ ♛ ♛ ♛ ♛ ♛ ♛ ♛ ♛ ♛ ♛ ♛ ♛

Later that night, I went to the club and as I walked around, I spotted Hester and Jade. I hadn't seen them since the night Kandi almost OD'd. I blamed them but truth was they didn't make Kandi get high and they didn't make her get in the car with Chaz. I just needed somebody to blame and they were there. I walked over to them and Hester looked like she was ready to fight.

I held up my hand. "Chill I ain't here to fight you."

Hester looked me up and down. "What do you want then?"

"I just wanted to make clear that there's no beef between us … unless that's what you want?" I paused and looked at both of them with a raised eyebrow. They didn't respond. "Good, I was upset about what happened to Kandi but that was no excuse for me to blame y'all for her actions."

Hester's facial expression softened. "We heard what happened to her. We didn't mean for that shit to go down. I mean, we're not a babysitter but we wouldn't set her up like that."

"That's good to know but you both know what shit can happen working here, especially to young girls up in here. If we don't look out for each other, these niggas certainly won't."

Hester nodded, "I hear you. Is Kandi coming

back?"

"No. She's going back to college. I'ma make sure she stays on track this time."

She smiled, "Good for her. You're a good person Jasmine. Too bad we all don't have you looking out for us." Hester told me and walked away with Jade.

For some reason it felt good hearing her say that to me. She was the fourth person to call me a good person this week. I wondered if they all were seeing something I wasn't? All this time I had been trying my best to be a "that bitch" and I ended up growing a heart instead. How the hell did that happen?

The club closed at two thirty so I decided to make my move up to Malachi's office. Bump, of course, stopped me at the steps.

"Wus up Jasmine?"

"Wus up Bump? Is Malachi up in his office?"

He nodded, "Yep."

"I need to see him."

"About what?"

I smirked, "Business."

He smirked back. He knew exactly what I meant. Half the time I bet he had his ear to the door listening to Malachi and I conduct business. He took out his cell phone and called him.

"What's in there?" he asked, pointing toward my large shoulder bag.

"Nothing much." I opened it for him to take a peek inside.

"C'mon." He hung up the phone, and I followed him.

Bump opened the door and I saw Malachi in his chair smoking a cigar and looking over some paperwork.

Bump left and closed the door behind him.

"Jasmine if you ain't here to fuck then I can't be bothered," Malachi said still pissed about the shit I said to him last time.

"Well then, I guess I'll leave and keep this information I got about Don P to myself." I turned and walked toward the door.

"Wait. What information?"

I turned back around and took a seat in the chair in front of his desk. I looked at the paperwork he had on his desk, then refocused my gaze on him. "I found out from a very reliable source who this Don P is and where he is."

"From who?" Malachi questioned. He noticed me looking at the papers strewn on his desk. He gathered them then turned them over.

I smiled at him. "Nikki."

Malachi frowned, "Nikki? What did she tell you?"

"Well before we discuss that we need to discuss how much this information is worth to you." I rubbed my fingers together.

"Hmp. Depending if it's good information it could be very profitable for you."

"Profitable as in $100,000?"

Malachi scowled. "Don't try and romp wit me. I'll give you $50,000 if it's true. Do we have a deal?"

I smiled, "That sounds good to me. Where's the cash?"

Malachi sighed, leaned to his left and opened the safe underneath his desk. I noticed he quickly put the papers he had on his desk into the safe, but then he pulled out a couple of stacks and threw them on the desk in front of me. I recognized the band colors that held the money.

I quickly put the money in my large shoulder bag but then I realized it was only half. "Malachi, this is only 25 g's," I said with a perplexed look on my face.

"Half now. The other half after I verify what you're saying to me is true. Now what did Nikki say to you?" Malachi scowled.

"Well, you know me and Nikki have gotten very close the past couple of weeks," I implied purposely.

"You have?" he replied, surprised. "And why haven't you told me about dat?"

"I never kiss and tell … well, unless I'm getting paid to."

He sucked his teeth, "Continue."

"Well, first of all, Nikki really hates you." Malachi scowled again at me and I laughed on the inside. "She trying to find any way she can to get away from you and she thinks she has. A couple of nights ago after we got done doing what we do, she shared with me just how she plans to do that."

He exhaled deeply, "What does dis have to do with Don P?"

"I'm getting to that part." I sighed. "She told me that she wanted me to kick it with her and her new man, Don P. So of course I'm shocked by this, because I don't just get down with any nigga, especially niggas beefing with you. Nikki told me he's going to take you out and they'll be running shit after you're dead."

Malachi looked at me suspiciously, "So why would you tell me this? Why not go with them and kill me?"

"I'm not gonna lie, it sounded tempting but then she told me that the man who's supposed to take you out and make this miracle come up is really that lame nigga Polo." I shook my head in disbelief. "I like the way things are now. I make lots of money being with you and it's better to deal with the devil I know than one I don't."

"Polo!" Malachi yelled angrily. "Dat nigga who's been trying to get down wit my crew is the same nigga trying to bloodclot kill me?!" Malachi slammed his fist on the desk and it felt like he almost cracked the thing in two. "Yuh sure about dis?"

I nodded with a smirk on my face. "Polo was Dre's best friend. He's always wanted Nikki for himself and he hates you for killing Dre. Personally I think you done him a favor cause now he's fucking Nikki day and night." I added for spite.

Malachi got up and slammed his fist down on his filing cabinet. I had never seen him that pissed before. I didn't know he wanted Nikki that bad. "No wonder she was so brave and tess mi. Her and Polo trying to kill mi … pussyholes." He turned and glared at me and for the first time I was afraid for myself. Maybe this wasn't as simple as I thought it would be. "Where are they?"

"I don't exactly know where they're held up at. Nikki been ghost the past couple of days but she did tell me that Polo has a big deal going down tonight in Hapeville off of Airport Loop Road and Forrest Avenue. The old storage warehouse around 4 am. Something about finding an out of state connect."

"Pussyholes," he mumbled again, "they want to bloodclot play with me?" Malachi picked up his phone, "Get Ricky and Reggie up here now," he ordered Bump and hung up. I sat nervously in the chair trying not to turn Malachi's wrath toward me. I could literally see the veins in his head protrude as he paced his office. A few seconds later Bump opened the door with Ricky and

Reggie behind him. Reggie had bandages on his head from the ass kicking Malachi gave him a few days ago.

"What's up Malachi?" Ricky asked.

"I just found out who this pussyhole Don P is." He glared at Reggie, "It's dat nigga Polo." Both Reggie and Ricky were shocked by his words.

"What? Naw, that's not possible," Reggie said scared to death. "I mean how could he be?"

Malachi back-handed him across the face, "Yuh dummy ya wutless! He's been using yuh to get close to me. If you weren't such a fucking idiot yuh would have realized it."

He held his face. "But Mala, he was the one who shot Dre for you," Reggie explained.

"The nigga I told yuh to kill," Malachi screamed. "He mash up Dre because he wanted Nikki and now that pussyhole wants to take my spot. Ricky get my niggas ready for war now. We're going to Hapeville to pay Polo a bumbaclot visit."

"Right away," Ricky replied and walked out. Reggie turned to follow him.

"Where da bumbaclot yuh think you're going?" Malachi yelled at him.

The fear Reggie had on his face was like that of an abused wife. "I ... I ... was going with Rick."

"Yuh ain't going anywhere!" Malachi grabbed him by the collar and yanked his ass back. "I got other things for yuh to do!"

"Okay, okay," Reggie timidly replied.

"You're going to stay here and watch her." Malachi pointed to me.

I crinkled my eyebrows, "What? I got things to do."

Malachi turned and grabbed the back of the chair I

was in and got in my face. His breath was hot and the look in his eyes was that of pure rage. "Yuh don't got shit to do until I come back here with Polo's blood on my shoes. Then yuh'll get paid the rest of your money. And if you're lying I'll put you in a hole right next to dat bitch Nikki when I catch her ass." He turned and walked up on Reggie. "Watch her. If she tries to leave shoot her in the leg." He put his finger in his face. "Don't fuck dis up."

"Yeah Mala, I g ... g ... got you," Reggie stuttered.

Malachi looked at Bump, "Let's go."

The two marched out of the office and Reggie stood guard over me. This was not how it was supposed to go. I could only pray that Polo killed Malachi because if he doesn't Malachi would kill Nikki and maybe me too for the hell of it.

Chapter Twenty-One

I'm Going In and I'ma Go Hard

Hapeville, GA
Malachi

You try and murder me, I will murder yuh. Finding out that this little pussyhole Polo was the one behind trying to murder me wasn't surprising. I didn't trust any nigga, but to find out Nikki had been fucking him all this time was unacceptable and disrespectful. Although this info coming from Jasmine was a bit suspicious, Reggie confirmed that Polo shot Dre which validated her claim … for now. I knew first hand that Nikki's pussy was good enough to kill for. Jasmine had loyalty to nothing but money, that was why I left Reggie behind to watch her. If she was telling the truth then I'd pay her. If not, I had a bullet with her name on it.

In less than thirty minutes Ricky had gotten together a group of niggas 20 deep and ready for war. I was going to oversee this shit myself so no mistakes would be made. I wanted to kill that pussyhole Polo, but before I did, I wanted to find out where Nikki was. I had special plans for her. She was going to feel my dick one last time before I murdered her.

I rode in a custom armored black Hummer, filled with artillery and weapons. I was armed with my Mac 11 and 45 Magnum cocked and ready to send people to their maker. Bump drove and Ricky was in the car right behind us. I had done business in Hapeville in the past and knew the perfect spot was over by Airport Loop Road. There were a few secluded areas to conduct business. As we pulled up, I didn't see anything. We parked outside of the warehouse and I motioned for Ricky to check it out. Ricky and Chaz got out of the car and ran up to the warehouse with guns in hand to assess the situation. I sat on the passenger's side of the Hummer and watched them move around the building. Moments later, they headed back and Ricky shook his head letting me know the spot was empty.

Shit! If dat bitch Jasmine was lying to me I'll make sure her ass doesn't see the sun rise! I thought to myself. Just as I was about to signal for us to pull out, a barrage of gunshots rang out. Chaz was the first one to get cut down. His chest was torn open by hot slugs. I turned and saw a group of niggas approaching us from the next building on foot. I ducked out of the Hummer and returned fire with my Mac 11 spraying them pussyholes up. I hit two, maybe three, niggas as my crew scrambled around their cars taking fire. We were taken off guard. A few of my niggas got hit.

Then I spotted Polo and I opened fire on his bumbaclot ass. "Mash dem up!" I yelled as I busted my Mac 11.

"I got ya Boss." Bump went into the backseat of the Hummer and pulled out a rocket launcher. He rested it on his shoulder, and locked his sights on Polo behind the crates. Bump fired the rocket and a stream of smoke cut through the sky as niggas ran for their lives. An explosion erupted. Niggas and debris flew through the air.

"I got 'em boss," Bump yelled as he took aim again, but before he could fire again a bullet tagged him in the shoulder and he fell to the ground. My niggas flanked to the right of us trying to surround us. I jumped back in the armored Hummer, protected from the gunfire. I looked out the back and saw Ricky get hit in the head by a bullet. I closed my eyes in disbelief as I watched him go down. This was turning into a blood bath for us. We were outnumbered. They were waiting for us. This wasn't a drug deal this was a fucking set up!

Now it was all about survival. My niggas were either dead or injured and they were closing in on me. I knew that nigga Polo must have gotten hit or at least some shrapnel from that rocket blast. I had to get out of there. The keys to the Hummer were still in the ignition and I ducked down and started the beast. I glanced over and saw Bump still alive but in pain on the ground on his back. He grabbed the rocket launcher and aimed it at the niggas closing in and fired again. Another explosion erupted and body parts hit the ground like we were in Iraq. He gave me the opening I needed. I mashed down on the gas and ran over a nigga who was thrown to the ground after the blast. I busted through the metal fence and onto the road. Gunshots bounced off of the Hummer as I took off down the street. I made it and the only thing on my mind was vengeance. That bitch Jasmine was going to pay wit her life for dis shit!

Jasmine

This was not how this shit was supposed to go down. It had been almost an hour since Malachi left me with Reggie watching over me in his office. The club was empty and closed for business. I knew I couldn't just sit and wait for whatever to happen. My phone had been vibrating in my purse but I couldn't dare check it. Reggie was the key to my freedom. He sat in Malachi's chair eyeing me up and down while texting on his phone.

"So how long are you going to let Malachi bully you like this?" I asked him.

"Shut up."

"Is that your response? C'mon Reggie how do you ever expect to be your own man if you keep on letting Malachi treat you like his little bitch?"

Reggie glared at me, "I ain't his bitch!"

"I can't tell. Reggie what do you really have for yourself?" I leaned forward and asked him. "Malachi has it all … and what do you have? Free access to the girls locker room," I said sarcastically.

"You think he really owns the place?" he snapped angrily. "Malachi just runs shit! But I'ma get mines!"

"Whateva nigga," I dismissed. "How you gonna do that with Malachi's foot in your ass all the time?"

"He's my brother and he looks out for me, but you'll see."

I chuckled, "Is that what you call it? That was fucked up what he did to you in here the other day. Why did he go off like that?" I asked playing dumb. I knew Malachi whooped his ass because I told him what Reggie tried to do to Nikki.

"None of your business! And if you think you can talk your way out of here ... forget it!" he yelled.

I sighed and leaned back. If he had half a brain he would've listened to me and we could've cut a deal and got out of here with some money. I knew Malachi had a fortune in the safe underneath his desk. I sat there for another five minutes not saying a word but then it hit me that I had been trying to get at Reggie the wrong way. His weakness had always been pussy and he had wanted mine for months. I was wearing a white mini skirt, a pink low cut midriff top tee shirt that just covered my titties, and a crop and fitted motorcycle jacket.

I stood up and took off my jacket, "Mind if I get comfortable?"

Reggie stopped texting and eyed me up and down and smiled. "Go right ahead."

I tossed my jacket on the sofa behind me and sat back down in the chair. Reggie's eyes were glued to my body. I leaned back and opened my legs then placed my hand in between my legs and started touching myself. I bit my bottom lip, closed my eyes, and leaned my head back.

"What are you doing?" Reggie asked.

"I'm relaxing."

He stood up to get a better view of what I was doing. "That's how you relax?"

I stared at him. "I'm bored and horny. I just need to bust a nut and I'll be good."

Reggie walked around from the desk and watched me. He grabbed his dick. "Need any help catching that nut?"

I stared at him for a second as if I was contemplating it and shrugged my shoulders. Reggie came toward me quickly, got on his knees, and slid his hands up my thighs and touched my pussy. "Damn you wet."

I gave him a moan letting him think I enjoyed his touch. Reggie bent down and kissed my legs. I pushed him back, stood up and sat on top of Malachi's desk. I leaned back and opened my legs and Reggie stood between my thighs. He reached up my skirt and pulled down my thong exposing my fat pussy lips to him. "Damn, I always loved the way that pussy looked on stage but it looks so much better up close."

"Why don't you give it a kiss?" I purred.

That was only a word. Reggie smiled and went down on me. He licked, sucked, and slurped my pussy. The little ugly muthafucka could eat some pussy real good. It was actually feeling good, and to my surprise, I came in his mouth. Reggie was getting into it but before he thought I was going to let him stick his dick in me I spied Malachi's marble ashtray on his desk. Reggie continued to dig his tongue in deeper and pulled me forward, making me his early morning meal. I contemplated getting another nut off, but instead, I reached out and grabbed the ashtray. With as much force as I could, I cracked Reggie upside his head. His head bounced off the desk and he hit the floor knocked the fuck out.

I jumped up and looked at him laid out on the floor. I shook my head, always a sucker for pussy. I grabbed my thongs and put them back on then frisked Reggie, and pulled out his gun. I walked back around Malachi's desk and spotted his safe. I wasn't no safe cracker but I knew how to fire a gun pretty good. I took Reggie's Glock 23 and aimed it at the safe lock and fired. I jerked back. The lock had a hole in it but it was not open. I blasted it again and it gave way. I grabbed my black bag and started filling it with rubber banded stacks of money. It must have been at least $200,000 in there. I hit the jackpot. As I was emptying the safe, I spotted some documents and I took them out. Sitting down in Malachi's chair, I looked them over. I was shocked at what I saw. I remembered him looking at paperwork before so this must have been it. It was a quitclaim deed to The Pink Palace. My eyes lit up. I saw the name Leroy Love Jr. signed on the deed but not Malachi's. So what Reggie told me was true. Legally Malachi didn't own The Pink Palace. Actually, nobody did. I always wanted my own business and this was my way to come up and own one over night. I may not have been a safe cracker but I was always good at reading legal documents.

Then I took the quitclaim deed and signed my name on it, under Leroy's, effectively putting The Pink Palace in my name. This wasn't a fair exchange, this was robbery! Besides, Malachi was either going to be dead or in jail sooner than later. I may as well run shit.

I quickly folded the paperwork and put it in the bag with the money. I dropped the Glock 23 in the bag and zipped it up. As I start walking out of the office, the door flew open and a gun was pointed in my face.

Andre "Dre" Wade

Jayson and I had a bird's eye view of the mayhem

that went down in front of the warehouse. Both Malachi and Polo were gunning for each other and just like we planned they fell for it. Jayson got on his radio and called it in and cops would arrive soon. Jayson also sent them to The Pink Palace in case Malachi showed up there. There were plenty of men either dead or injured all around the warehouse but then I spotted a green and orange Pontiac speeding away from the scene and I knew it was Polo.

"Jay, that's Polo! I'm going after him."

Jayson looked at me and knew what I was going to do to him, "Be careful."

I nodded and jumped in Jayson's car and took off after him. Within minutes I caught up to him as he turned onto the highway. If I were him I would have been getting the hell out of Atlanta but he turned onto I-285 East and I followed behind him. He was pushing it, doing at least 80 mph until he exited off onto 69, Old National Highway in College Park. The son of a bitch was heading to my house to see Nikki. He must have known she set him up. But little did he know she wasn't there. She was at the safe house waiting for me. The traitor tried to kill me and tried to steal my woman.

Soon he turned off of Old National into the Stone Ridge subdivision and was heading toward my house. I took a back road so he wouldn't see me coming. I cut my lights and parked down the street. I made sure my 45 was locked and loaded and I jumped out of the car and cut through my neighbor's yard hopping the fence. I saw Polo at my back door and he kicked it in. I made a mental note to myself to get a storm door for the back. I followed him in and I heard him upstairs.

"Nikki! Nikki! Where are you bitch? I'ma kill yo

ass!"

He was going room to room looking for her. It was dark and I waited in the kitchen with my gun in hand for him to come back downstairs. Polo jogged back down the stairs and froze in his tracks when he saw me pointing my gun at his head. My face was still concealed by darkness.

"Whoa, hey … I live here," he lied.

"You wish you did nigga," I said coldly.

Polo's mouth opened instantly, "Dre … is that you?"

I took a step forward so he could see my face, "Who else would it be?"

He looked like he saw a ghost when he saw me. "But you … you're s'posed to be …"

"Dead? You need to work on your aim nigga. If you shoot a nigga you better make sure he's dead. I thought I taught you better than that, but you were never a fast learner were you?"

A panicked expression washed over his face, "Dre, Malachi … made me do it. He … he said if I didn't he would send somebody to wipe out you and your whole family."

"Oh, so you did the humane thing instead and shot me in the fucking back in front of my girl and my kid?" I spat angrily. "You wanted Nikki so bad that you tried to murder me to get to her?"

"Dre, c'mon man," he pleaded with me, sweating, like a runaway slave. "We can work something out here. Listen, we can kill Malachi and take over his shit. We can run this shit together!"

I chuckled, "You such a bitch ass nigga. I can't believe I ever called you my friend." I shook my head.

"We set you up nigga. Nikki and I have been playing you this whole time. Malachi was supposed to kill you tonight by the warehouse but I guess you being the cockroach that you are you slipped through the cracks. Doesn't matter because I'd rather kill your ass myself."

Polo dropped to his knees with fear in his eyes. "Please Dre! Don't do this man! I'm your nigga! We boys!"

For half a second I felt pity for him and in that second of hesitation on my part Polo raised his gun and took a shot at me hitting the wall next to my head. I busted back hitting him dead in his chest right through his heart. Polo jerked back then looked at me in shock before his eyes rolled back in the back of his head. The gun dropped from his hand. He slumped over on the floor as a pool of blood formed underneath him. I walked up to him and kicked his gun out of reach.

"I told you to work on your aim nigga."

Chapter Twenty-Two

Battle of the Sexes

Atlanta, GA
Nikki

I had been calling Jasmine for over an hour and she hadn't picked up. After I kept getting her voicemail I called Gina and she told me that Jasmine went up to Malachi's office; then a few minutes later, Malachi and his niggas raised up outta the club. Gina told me she was getting ready to leave for the night but Jasmine was still in the office with Reggie. That sent chills up my spine. Not only was Jasmine still up there, but also she was with that wannabe rapist, which was even more frightening.

Before I got off the phone with Gina, she assured me

she would leave the back door open when she locked up. I knew it was going to be dangerous but I had to go there. Jasmine was in a dangerous situation because of me and I wasn't going to leave her there. I made sure I was packing the .9mm Dre had given me and I was off to The Pink Palace. Twenty minutes later I arrived and parked in the lot then went to the back entrance. The door was unlocked like Gina said it would be.

I took my 9mm out of my bag and crept inside. It was dark. I looked up toward Malachi's office and saw a shimmer of light through the closed blinds. Chances were Reggie was armed and I would probably need to shoot his ass. I had no problem doing that. I went up the stairs and stood still, listening for any sounds. I heard none. Then with my hand out, and gun extended ready to blast, I took a deep breath and quickly opened the door with my free hand. To my surprise I saw Jasmine heading toward me with a black bag over her shoulder.

"Oh shit!" Jasmine yelled.

"Oh God!" I exhaled, "I thought you were in trouble." I lowered the gun and put it back in my bag.

"I was but it wasn't nothing I couldn't handle. Girl you nearly gave me a heart attack," she said, relieved.

I spotted Reggie knocked the fuck out on the floor with a big knot on his head. "Damn, what the hell happened to him?"

Jasmine glanced back. "His dumb ass was just another sucker for pussy," she chuckled.

I smiled. "Let's get the hell outta here!"

We made our way downstairs and I noticed her bag seemed heavy. "So you got paid, huh?"

"That and then some," Jasmine confirmed. As we turned the corner Jasmine got hammered and flew into a wall. She dropped to the floor like a rag doll, unconscious. I turned around and saw Malachi with a gun in his hand and a menacing glare on his face. He looked like he just come back from a battlefield. His suit was soiled and he was sweaty.

"Bitch," he growled and grabbed me by the neck. Instantly he began to choke the shit out of me. He picked me up by my neck and I couldn't breathe. "I'm gonna to kill your bumbaclot ass!" He tossed me onto a tabletop and my bag with my gun dropped to the floor out of my reach. He was on top of me choking me so hard that I couldn't even move. A sting shot across my face when he slapped me. "Yuh wanna bloodclot fuck wit me? Well I'ma fuck yuh!"

He grabbed my belt buckle and tried to take it off. I tried to fight back but he hit me again stunning me momentarily. I was no match for him physically but then I remembered my other weapon. Just as he was unbuttoning my pants, I reached into my jacket pocket and pulled out my razor blade. In one swoop, I slashed Malachi across the face. The force made blood skeet across the floor.

"Aarrrrrrgh," he yelled and grabbed the side of his face giving me a moment to roll off the table and run. "BITCH!" Malachi screamed and I heard thunder explode behind me. Three shots nearly missed me. I headed toward the back near the locker rooms. As I ran, I saw a baseball bat in the corner that the security guys used as extra reinforcement when somebody got too rowdy. I grabbed it.

I could hear Malachi turning over tables coming after me. It was dark so that gave me a chance to hide behind the rows of lockers.

"I'm going to kill yuh bitch," he roared and my heart beat like a jackhammer in my chest. "Once I kill yuh, then I'm gonna to find that pickney of yours and slit his throat!"

His threat against my child pissed me off and if I made it out of here alive he would be dead from my bare hands. But for the time being, I had to be cool. I wasn't going to give Malachi what he wanted and he wanted me to yell back at him so he could find me, but I stayed silent.

"I was going to give yuh da world Nikki ... I was going to make yuh wifey," he said out loud. "But yuh betrayed me! Try to kill me!" I heard his footsteps come closer. "Now yuh gonna bloodclot die!"

I readied myself because I knew I maybe had one chance. His footsteps were much closer and I heard him breathing hard. As quietly as I could, I slipped around the locker but was met with the barrel of his gun, just inches away. I took the bat and swung for the fences!

"Aarrgh," Malachi yelled. He dropped the gun and it slid across the floor. I could tell by the cracking sound I must have broken some digits. I jumped from behind the locker and swung like A-Rod for Malachi's head. The mutherfucka ducked and I bashed the lockers but he punched me in the jaw. The force not only sent me flying into the lockers behind me but forced the bat out of my hand. My jaw hurt like hell but I had no time to acknowledge it cause Malachi grabbed the bat off the floor and I took off running backstage. I heard him right behind me closing in.

"Aarragh," I yelled, feeling a blunt object whack into the back of my leg. The force sent me flying forward, sliding onto the main club stage. Malachi threw the bat at me. I hit the stage floor hard and felt pain all over me. I looked back and saw Malachi pick up the bat. I started to crawl away but Malachi quickly walked up on me.

"I'm gonna bash yuh pretty little head in," he yelled and raised the bat over his head. He swung downward, but before he could hit, me a thunderous explosion erupted in the club sending Malachi flying backward, crashing on the stage floor. I turned and looked and saw Jasmine holding a gun in her hands.

"I always wanted to shoot him," Jasmine said. She ran toward me and jumped up on the stage. "Are you okay?"

I exhaled and smiled, "I am … thanks to you."

"I owed you one." She helped me up and I put my arm around her shoulder. We both looked at Malachi's body on the floor.

"Is he dead?" she asked.

I looked closely and saw his chest moving, "No. Looks like you hit him in his stomach."

"Well, I was aiming for his head."

"We'll work on your aim later. Are you okay?"

Jasmine touched her head. "I got one hell of a headache but I'm fine."

Jasmine helped me off the stage and we sat down in chairs. We heard the sound of sirens resonating in the background. A few minutes later Atlanta PD came barreling in through the back door. I had never been happier to see a shitload of cops.

Epilogue

Meet me at the altar in your white dress

Atlanta, GA
Malachi

I felt pain like I had never felt before. My mouth was dry, my body sore, and I didn't know where I was. I looked around and realized I was in a hospital bed and then I felt handcuffs around my wrists and I'm handcuffed to the bed railing. I spot two police guards standing at my door, and a nurse checking my vitals.

I try and speak, "Wa ... water."

The nurse jumps noticing that I'm awake, "Yes," she said and poured some water in a pitcher into a Styrofoam cup and then put it to my lips. I sip as much as I could. "We didn't expect you to wake up so early after surgery."

"Surgery," I repeat, "Where am I?"

"You're at Grady Memorial Hospital. You just had surgery to remove the bullet from your abdomen five hours ago."

I remember. I was about to kill that bitch Nikki and that other bitch Jasmine shot me. Then I saw a bag next to me. "What's dat?"

"That's a colostomy bag Mr. Turner. The bullet destroyed your colon," she explained. "You should get some rest."

"Rest? I'm shitting into a bag for the rest of my life and I should get some rest!"

She stepped away from the bed and the guards step closer. I was in no condition to fight so I lie back. "I wanna call my lawyer."

♛ ♛ ♛ ♛ ♛ ♛ ♛ ♛ ♛ ♛ ♛ ♛ ♛ ♛ ♛ ♛ ♛

Two hours later my lawyer Jerry Powell comes to my hospital room. He was a white man who I used to beat any charges brought up against me. He was the best at what he does. For the amount I paid him per hour he had better be. He ordered the guards out of the room for a private talk.

"So what am I looking at?" I ask him.

"It's not good Malachi. They have a lot of physical evidence against you. Not to mention Ms. Bell and Ms. Dawson are willing to testify that you attacked them in her club."

I scrunch my eyebrows, "Her club? What the bloodclot are yuh talking about! That's my club!"

"She has a quitclaim deed that lists her as the

owner."

"Dat bitch! I never gave her my club!" I sat up and leaned closer to Jerry.

"She has documented proof that the club is hers."

"I don't care what—"

"Malachi, calm down. Regardless of who owns the club, that's the least of your concerns right now," Jerry explained.

"What do you mean?"

"The DA office has got a star witness willing to turn states evidence against you. They're looking to prosecute you on RICO law. It provides them the ability to prosecute you under extended criminal penalties and civil cause of action for acts performed as leader of an ongoing criminal organization," Jerry explained.

"Who is their witness?"

Jerry swallowed hard, "Mr. Reginald Turner. Your brother."

Jasmine

I guess Reggie finally got tired of being Malachi's bitch and turned states evidence against that nigga. I'm sure he figured the witness protection program was better than 25 to 30 years in prison any day. I worked with the police and gave them my story of Malachi attacking Nikki and me. They ate it up. With the charges he was facing he didn't have time to worry about my club.

The best part of this whole situation is that with the money I got from Malachi I was able to completely pay off Kandi's college tuition at Clark. Now she could just go to school and not worry about anything other than getting her degree.

Besides, the money I'm now making from The Pink Palace is more then enough to make up the difference. After being closed for three weeks I reopened the club under new management. Not only was the reopening a big hit but also I was now getting the respect from everybody as a businesswoman. I even made Hester the den mother of the club and it was her job to look at after the girls and make sure they weren't taken advantage of by anyone. My days of dancing on the stage were over. The only person I was dancing for was Chauncey. Yes we're still dating and dare I say it? I love him.

I've started talking to my father again after the encouragement of Chauncey, Kandi, and my mother. We're now taking baby steps in reconnecting as father and daughter. After my parents found out I was the club owner and not a dancer anymore they felt a lot better.

I've learned a lot by becoming friends with Nikki over the last few months. I felt like she's a sister I could confide in whenever I need somebody to talk to. We're very like-minded in a lot of ways. Today I closed The Pink Palace to the public because I was having a private party for my new friends, Nikki and Dre. Well not just a party, it was their wedding reception!

Nikki

I can't believe how nervous I am today. It felt like this day was never going to come but after we cleared things up with the whole Polo and Malachi mess the first thing Dre wanted to do was marry me. After Dre killed Polo's snake ass he called Jayson and he was the first officer on the scene. Because Polo broke into our home and fired his gun at Dre, the police said his killing was in self defense and no charges were brought up against him.

Malachi was convicted under RICO law for running a criminal organization and murder and was sentenced to 25 to life in federal prison. His brother Reggie was the prosecution's star witness and this nigga told everything. Despite what everyone thought, he wasn't that dumb. He's probably now living in Montana on a farm in the witness protection program.

But today was my day. My wedding day and everybody was in attendance at our church in College Park. Janelle was of course my maid of honor and Penny, Jasmine and Kandi were my bridesmaids. Jayson was Dre's best man and even little Tyler was one of his daddy's groomsmen. The time was finally here and I took the long walk down the aisle in my white lace Vera Wang dress. Dre looked like a king in his Sean John tuxedo waiting for me.

"I, Nicole Bell, take you Andre Wade, to be my husband, to have and to hold from this day forward, for better or for worse, for richer, for poorer, in sickness and in health, to love and to cherish; from this day forward until death do us part," I said with a tear tugging my eye.

The preacher looked at Dre, "You may now place the ring on her finger."

Dre slid the ring on my finger, "I, Andre Wade, take you Nicole Bell, to be my wife, to have and to hold from this day forward, for better or for worse, for richer, for poorer, in sickness and in health, to love and to cherish; from this day forward until death do us part."

The preacher looked at us and smiled. "Well I guess there is only one thing for me to say: Andre and Nicole by the powers vested in me by God and the State of Georgia, I now pronounce you man and wife. You may kiss your beautiful bride!"

Dre lifts my veil and gave me the sweetest kiss I've ever felt. I can't believe that I'm now Mrs. Nicole Wade. This is the happiest day of my life.

Acknowledgements

What's up everybody! Well, I'm back again for the first time. It funny how things come full circle and I'm happy to bring y'all this second installment of *The Pink Palace* here on Triple Crown Publications where it all started.

So some of you may ask why a sequel? Honestly, when I wrote the first *Pink Palace*, I had no intention of doing another follow up book. At the time when I was writing the first one I was just worried about getting through it and having it make sense. It wasn't 'till after the book came out that folks started asking me when is the next Pink Palace coming out? I was like "What, who, next?" So I stayed away from it at first and said if enough people ask me for it and I can think of a good enough story I'll do it. So over the last two years you guys did ask for this. So you forced me to think of what the hell could get these girls back in the strip club again? But I didn't want to tell the same story over again. I wanted this book to be familiar but very different then the first. So after months of thinking, discussions with my wife, and a fifth of Jack Daniels I took to my keyboard and this is what came out. Hope you like it.

So there's a few people I need to thank for making this book a reality. My wife Sheena, there's nobody I trust more. Without you telling me, "What's this crap? That's whack! Write it again!" I never would have got this book right. LOL... I love you boo.

Cynthia Mocha Jones, the best editor in the world. Thank you for not killing me for all my typos, grammatical errors, run on sentences, and the annoying uses of the words, "towards" "forwards" or "hazel eyes"... I'm saving them all for the next book! Smile. I can't thank you enough for all you have done. Can't wait to read your book!

Raequel Edgerson, my writing partner. Folks are gonna be shocked when they see what we've been cooking up! Thank you for being more like family than a friend. *Diary Confessions* and *Use To Temporary Happiness* is coming!

Jarold Imes, thank you for believing in my work and me when everything was going wrong. Continue to be successful my friend. K. Roland Williams and Ben Blaze my brothers of the pen. Keep on dropping the hottest books! When one of us succeeds we all do. To my homies, Jamal "Jay" Smith and Kimeke Walker thanks for giving me a voice at VVC Radio. Destiny Carter, thanks for the hot interviews! (Go Yankees) Renita M. Walker, my sister of the pen. Keep doing your thing! Priscilla V. Sales, like I said before I can never thank you enough. You taught me well.

My family, love you mommy. Love you dad. Michael McCaulsky my brother rest in peace. To my sisters, Sandra and Joanne McCaulsky and brother Trevor McCaulsky. To my niece Kendra McCaulsky and her family. My family in St. Petersburg, FL, Jamaica, and England love you all. Rashida, Charelene, Adam, (Bigga) Daniel, and Joan. My second mother Beatrice Campbell (mum). Sharon Campbell and Shaun Campbell. Kaisha and Rhianna Campbell. Catriona Mills, Audrey Spencer, Ebony Spencer, Myrtle Clarke, Paige Woodhouse, Selena Fearon, Charlene Brown, Samantha Watts, Sharm Campbell and Tara Tweede. See you all soon.

Okay and a very special thank you to my reader extraordinaires who read *Pink Palace 2* first errors and all Shanequa 'BK' Pickering and Yolanda 'Lala' Mickles. Your feedback was priceless! Thanks for the thumbs up! To Lula Carter and Cherron Gilmore thank you for always supporting me. My author friends, Erica McNair, Jessica Terry, Jean Holloway, LaShaun Wright-Phillips, Victoria V. Anderson, Tu-Shonda L. Whitaker, Deja King, Juanita Ramos, and Tracy Brown.

The fam, Tamar Humes, Jeneise Humes, Mikiena Malcolm aka Gooduus, George Heath McKinney my best friend, Damaris DeJesus, Krystal Robinson, Tanya Bonilla, Tamara & Grenville Beatties, Alberto 'Tito' and Yaritza 'Yari' Ramos, Nadia Iris Bailey, and Latoya Arnold.

All the book clubs, What's Da Story, Marcus Williams at Nubian Bookstore, Medu Bookstore in Atlanta thank you for your support.

Vickie M. Stringer, thank you for once again

extending me your hand and giving me a platform to present my work. Without you this project would not be here now. I love seeing a strong black woman succeed in this business. Continue to be successful my sister.

Okay I'm tired now. If I forgot you, I'll catch you on the next one.

P.S. – Thank you to all of my supporters but if you hated the first *Pink Palace...* you're gonna really hate this one! Much love!

Marlon McCaulsky

♕ Triple Crown Publications

Order Form

P.O. Box 247378   Columbus, OH 43224

Name	
Address	
City	
State	Zipcode

QTY	TITLES	PRICE
	A Down Chick	$15.00
	A Hood Legend	$15.00
	A Hustler's Son	$15.00
	A Hustler's Wife	$15.00
	A Project Chick	$15.00
	Always a Queen	$15.00
	Amongst Thieves	$15.00
	Baby Girl	$15.00
	Baby Girl Pt. 2	$15.00
	Betrayed	$15.00
	Black	$15.00
	Black and Ugly	$15.00
	Blinded	$15.00
	Cash Money	$15.00
	Chances	$15.00
	China Doll	$15.00

Shipping & Handling
1 - 3 Books $5.00
4 - 9 Books $9.00
$1.95 for each add'l book

Total $_____

Forms of accepted payment: Unused Postage Stamps, Personal or Institutional Checks
& Money Orders. All mail in orders take 5-7 business days to be delivered.

♔ Triple Crown Publications

Order Form

P.O. Box 247378   Columbus, OH 43224

Name	
Address	
City	
State	Zipcode

QTY	TITLES	PRICE
	Chyna Black	$15.00
	Contagious	$15.00
	Crack Head	$15.00
	Crack Head II	$15.00
	Cream	$15.00
	Cut Throat	$15.00
	Dangerous	$15.00
	Dime Piece	$15.00
	Dirtier Than Ever	$20.00
	Dirty Red	$15.00
	Dirty South	$15.00
	Diva	$15.00
	Dollar Bill	$15.00
	Ecstasy	$15.00
	Flipside of the Game	$15.00
	For the Strength of You	$15.00

Shipping & Handling

1 - 3 Books $5.00
4 - 9 Books $9.00
$1.95 for each add'l book

Total $_____

Forms of accepted payment: Unused Postage Stamps, Personal or Institutional Checks & Money Orders. All mail in orders take 5-7 business days to be delivered.

♟ Triple Crown Publications

Order Form

P.O. Box 247378   Columbus, OH 43224

Name	
Address	
City	
State	Zipcode

QTY	TITLES	PRICE
	Game Over	$15.00
	Gangsta	$15.00
	Grimey	$15.00
	Hold U Down	$15.00
	Hood Richest	$15.00
	Hoodwinked	$15.00
	How to Succeed in the Publishing Game	$15.00
	Ice	$15.00
	Imagine This	$15.00
	In Cahootz	$15.00
	Innocent	$15.00
	Karma	$15.00
	Karma II	$15.00
	Keisha	$15.00
	Larceny	$15.00
	Let That Be the Reason	$15.00

Shipping & Handling
1 - 3 Books $5.00
4 - 9 Books $9.00
$1.95 for each add'l book

Total $_____

Forms of accepted payment: Unused Postage Stamps, Personal or Institutional Checks & Money Orders. All mail in orders take 5-7 business days to be delivered.

♕ Triple Crown Publications

Order Form

P.O. Box 247378 Columbus, OH 43224

Name	
Address	
City	
State	Zipcode

QTY	TITLES	PRICE
	Life	$15.00
	Love & Loyalty	$15.00
	Me & My Boyfriend	$15.00
	Menage's Way	$15.00
	Mina's Joint	$15.00
	Mistress of the Game	$15.00
	Queen	$15.00
	Rage Times Fury	$15.00
	Road Dawgz	$15.00
	Sheisty	$15.00
	Stacy	$15.00
	Stained Cotton	$15.00
	Still Dirty	$20.00
	Still Sheisty	$15.00
	Street Love	$15.00
	Sunshine & Rain	$15.00

Shipping & Handling
1 - 3 Books $5.00
4 - 9 Books $9.00
$1.95 for each add'l book

Total $_____

Forms of accepted payment: Unused Postage Stamps, Personal or Institutional Checks & Money Orders. All mail in orders take 5-7 business days to be delivered.

♕ Triple Crown Publications

Order Form

P.O. Box 247378   Columbus, OH 43224

Name	
Address	
City	
State	Zipcode

QTY	TITLES	PRICE
	The Cartel's Daughter	$15.00
	The Game	$15.00
	The Hood Rats	$15.00
	The Pink Palace	$15.00
	The Reason Why	$15.00
	The Set Up	$15.00
	Torn	$15.00
	Trickery	$15.00
	Vixen Icon	$15.00
	Whore	$15.00

Shipping & Handling
1 - 3 Books $5.00
4 - 9 Books $9.00
$1.95 for each add'l book

Total $_____

Forms of accepted payment: Unused Postage Stamps, Personal or Institutional Checks
& Money Orders. All mail in orders take 5-7 business days to be delivered.

Made in the USA
Lexington, KY
08 March 2011